The Door

By Donna Jay

Copyright © 2023 Donna Jay

Editor: Debbie McGowan

Acknowledgements

Heartfelt thanks go to my beta-readers, AC Miller, Lisa Caro & Cornelia Borner. Thanks also to my proofreaders and editor. This is a better book because of you all.

Chapter 1

With her divorce papers burning a hole in her handbag and her eyes drilling a hole through the neon-blue door, Eloise flicked her gaze higher. When her eyes landed on the sign, her stomach flipped.

Libellule's

Could she do this? Hell, yes.

She'd denied herself for years and refused to wait a day longer. Certain she would feel like a new woman by the time she left, Eloise took the final step. She rapped twice and waited.

The three seconds it took for the door to swing open felt like three hours.

"Come in." The woman's lips were as red as her sequined dress and painted nails. "Welcome to Libellule's. I'm Ruby."

"Hi. I'm Ally." It felt weird to say, but it was the first…second thing that came to her when she was asked what alias she would like to go by. The first name that came to mind was El, but it was too close to her online alias, and Taupō was a small place.

Eloise pushed the door closed behind her and took in her surroundings.

To her right, a woman was at a table having her nails painted. To her left, another woman sat on an oversized sofa, reading a magazine. A vase of flowers sat atop the counter, and a combination of scented candles and nail varnish perfumed the air.

To the casual observer, it looked like any other beauty parlour. If it hadn't been for a trusted ally and all the vetting Eloise had gone through — including being tested for STIs — she would've been second-guessing if she was in the right place.

A woman wearing a mauve tunic appeared in reception. "Demi?"

"Yep." The woman sitting on the sofa tossed her magazine on the table and disappeared into a room behind them.

Fuck. Eloise's stomach flipped. If the rooms were that close to everything else, she wasn't sure she could do this. What if the woman having a manicure heard her?

"Right this way," Ruby said.

Unable to back out now, Eloise followed her down a hallway. They came to a door that she'd assumed led outside, but she'd been mistaken. It opened up to an entirely different world. The scent out here was different. Spicy, like cinnamon and citrus.

A girl with her hair in pigtails wearing a schoolgirl outfit slipped past, keeping her gaze averted. Whether that was to respect Eloise's privacy or a sign of submission was anyone's guess.

The world of kink had always fascinated her, but the little she'd glimpsed of it had been in private, and she doubted what she'd seen online was a true indication of what went on in real life.

A door to the left near the end of the passageway opened, and a tall woman with long, black hair and alluring green eyes slowly appeared.

She was dressed completely in black—black corset, black miniskirt, black stockings and black high heels. And if that wasn't hot enough to set Eloise's body on fire, her captivating smile and the sleeve of tattoos covering her left arm did the trick.

Swallowing hard, Eloise did her best to remain composed, but she couldn't control the way her body reacted—the quaking of her heart, the throb between her legs.

"Ally, this is Savannah," Ruby said. "She'll take good care of you." With that, she turned and left them alone.

The door between the front and back of the business closed, sealing Eloise's fate. Only, it wasn't fate that put her here. She'd set the wheels in motion. Now, if only she could relax enough to enjoy the ride.

"This way." The woman—Savannah was it?—stepped aside, motioning for Eloise to enter the room. She had to be close to six foot tall, and her hair was so black it looked blue. Or maybe that was the blue light bulb casting the room in shadows.

Eloise didn't know where to look first, let alone where to put herself. Talk about sensory overload. A huge cross with anchor points on all four corners was against one wall, and an impressive assortment of implements hung off nearby hooks: paddle, flogger, crop, handcuffs, blindfold and something that looked like a badminton racket minus the netting.

"What's that?" Eloise nudged the handle with the tip of her finger as if it might bite.

"A twisted-loop spanking cane." Savannah took it off the hook and tapped it against her palm. "Stingy but with a wider pattern than your traditional cane." She hung it back up. "But I don't think you're ready for that."

"Oh, really?" Eloise straightened, trying not to let her uncertainty show.

Shooting her an amused look, Savannah reached for it. "Should we try?"

"Um, maybe not right away." Hell, she didn't even know what a paddle felt like.

The only impact play she'd had was too long ago to remember. When the other party wasn't into it, it just made her feel like a weirdo, so she'd never asked again.

Putting her ex out of her mind, she breathed in the heady scent of leather and stood there like an idiot. She was so far out of her league she might as well be sitting on the sideline.

"Let me take that." Savannah reached for her handbag. "Jacket too."

"Thank you." Eloise shrugged out of her coat and handed it over along with her bag.

"Nervous?"

"Terrified," she admitted. Was she supposed to just strip and stand there naked? Now that she was there, it all felt very…clinical.

"Let's talk." Savannah sat on what appeared to be a massage table pushed up against the wall. "Join me." She patted the spot beside her.

Being shorter than Savannah, Eloise braced her hands behind her and swung her backside up onto the bed.

"First time, huh?"

"Yep." She was pretty sure Savannah meant her first time exploring kink, so she didn't bother telling her it was also her first time with a woman.

If they were dating, she might've felt the need to do so, but they weren't, and that was why she was at Libellule's. She didn't want the complications that seemed to go hand in hand with a relationship.

Savannah pushed a lock of hair off Eloise's face. Terribly cliché, but, oh, so intimate.

"Firstly, we need to discuss your limits and a safe word."

How did you know your limits if you'd never explored? "Not the cane. Maybe not the flogger either." That looked painful. "Or the restraints, in case I freak."

Great. What did that leave? She might as well have stayed home.

"Safe word?" Savannah asked.

"Pickles." The reply came without thought.

"Not a fan?"

"Hate them," Eloise said.

"Okay, I don't think it'll come to it, but if you need to use that word, use it." With her gaze locked on Eloise, Savannah undid the top button on Eloise's blouse. The barely there brush of her fingers set Eloise's skin on fire.

She was doing this. Really doing it.

With a sexy gleam in her eye, Savannah pushed Eloise's blouse off her shoulders.

Her gaze was so intense it made Eloise feel like the most beautiful woman alive. Although it was all part of the illusion, she went with it, letting herself believe this gorgeous woman really wanted her.

When Savannah brushed a finger across the lacy fabric of Eloise's bra, her nipples hardened and warmth pooled between her thighs, already damp with arousal.

"Sensitive?"

"Very."

"Do the panties match your bra?"

"Of course." As if she would've worn mismatched underwear for such a monumental occasion.

Sizing her up like a black panther eyeing up its prey, Savannah stepped back. "Strip."

"Yes, Mistress." Where the hell had that come from? Embarrassed, Eloise scrambled to recover. "Sorry. Can I call you that?"

"You are delightful." She trailed a finger along Eloise's jaw. "And yes, you may."

"Thank you, Mistress." She unzipped her skirt and let it fall to the floor, loving the approving look Savannah cast her way.

She'd always done what she could to stay in shape, more for herself than anyone else, but she'd be lying if she said it didn't feel good right then to know Savannah appreciated it. The bra went next, but when she got to her briefs, she hesitated.

They were little more than a scrap of fabric, but she wasn't used to baring her pussy. Sex had always been with the lights off…under the covers.

Perfunctory and boring.

But she wanted this. God, she wanted this. So why was she hesitating?

"Leave them on…for now."

"How did you—"

"It's my job to read your body language. Besides, you look stunning in them."

Eloise basked in the praise. It'd been a long time since she'd been told she was beautiful, and it felt good, especially coming from this woman who looked like she wanted to eat her.

Oh, God. Her pulse throbbed between her legs. She hadn't meant it in the literal sense, but now that the thought was there, she couldn't let it go.

"Hands here." Savannah pointed to the top two anchor points on the cross in the corner of the room. "Feet here." She tapped the bottom two points with the toe of her shoe.

"I'm not sure about—"

"Do I need to gag you?"

"No!" Holy shit. No way. She wasn't down for that at all. To each their own, but she'd never seen the appeal. Well, she could for a dominant, but she wasn't the one issuing orders.

"Relax. But you need to trust me, okay?" Savannah held her gaze. Her expression was kind, not sadistic, putting Eloise at ease. "Good girl. Deep breath."

Eloise inhaled deeply.

"And out."

She did as she was told, instantly feeling calmer. She was way overthinking this and needed to stop. She also needed to throw away her preconceived ideas about how today would go.

"Let's try that again." Savannah tapped the four points on the cross. "Feet here. Hands here."

This time, without hesitation, Eloise parted her legs and put her arms above her head, mirroring an upright starfish as she plastered herself to the cross. The cool leather quickly heated, matching her body temperature.

"There are other ways of restraining people than with restraints," Savannah said. "One way is with my body." She plastered herself to Eloise's back, pushing her into the cross.

Basking in the feel of Savannah's corset against her naked flesh, Eloise closed her eyes, savouring the moment. She felt trapped but not afraid. When Savannah moved away, she immediately missed the contact. The temptation to spin around and ask Savannah to plaster herself to the front of her body was all-consuming, but the threat of a ball gag stopped her.

Actually, that wasn't entirely true. Even without any threats, she was ready to drop to her knees and worship this woman if she issued the command.

"Today I'm going to introduce you to honour bondage." Savannah's voice came from behind her. "Do you know what that is?"

She could hazard a guess, but why speculate when she had the perfect tutor? "No."

"It's when a dominant — me — trusts you not to move without permission." The crack of something echoed around the room. Ignoring the temptation to glance over her shoulder, Eloise kept her eyes straight ahead, staring through the cross at the wall before her.

"Can I trust you to do that?"

"Yes, Mistress."

"Good girl." A blindfold snapped into place and the room fell dark. "This will help you clear your mind and allow yourself to simply feel."

Knowing she was at Savannah's mercy was equally thrilling and nerve-wracking.

Fingertips raked down her back, making gooseflesh pop on her skin. She shivered, shoulders lifting, arms above her head, hands still gripping the D-rings on the corners of the cross.

"Delightful." Savannah's voice was little more than a purr. Next, something featherlike trailed down her arms, across her back and down her legs, waking up her senses.

"What's that?" Alarmed, Eloise's eyes flew open behind the blindfold. "Am I allowed to ask questions?"

"I'll allow that...today." Her throaty chuckle pulled a smile from Eloise. "It's a flogger. They're great not only for discipline but also for sensation play."

"Oh," Eloise said lamely. She probably should've known that, considering her online application stated she wanted to explore bondage and discipline.

The strands of the flogger landed across her backside, making her gasp. It hadn't hurt, but the unexpected blow took her by surprise. Pleasantly by surprise. Her backside tingled, and she welcomed the new sensation.

The strands danced across her flesh again. "I also like to use the traffic-light system. Green for go. Yellow for slow—"

"Red for stop," Eloise said. She knew that much, at least.

"Or in your case, pickles."

"Oh, yeah." She laughed.

"Something funny?" Another blow landed.

This one had more bite, but again, it wasn't unpleasant. If anything, the lick of heat was arousing. More so than she'd anticipated. "No, Mistress."

"Good girl." Savannah pulled on the waistband of Eloise's underwear, lowering them to the crease of her arse.

Behind the blindfold, Eloise conjured up an image of herself standing in a submissive pose, backside exposed, silently begging for more. She wiggled her hips, earning herself another crack.

"Some dominants don't reward bad behaviour, but I'm rather fond of brats. Gives me a reason to punish them." She struck again.

Eloise sucked in a sharp breath, back bowing. It wasn't that she wanted to get away from the sting, but she wasn't there just to be thrashed either.

Savannah put a hand on her shoulder. "Turn around."

Feeling disorientated, Eloise let go of the D-rings she'd been gripping and fumbled blindly.

"I've got you." The feel of Savannah's breath on her neck sent a shiver up her spine.

As she pivoted, cool air hit Eloise's sternum, and her backside touched the warm leather behind her.

"How are your arms?"

"Heavy." She had no idea how long she'd been standing spreadeagled, but now that she'd lowered her arms, they felt fatigued.

"Would you like more sensation play?"

"I would really like to kiss you." Shit, where had that come from? Were you allowed to kiss sex workers? "So—"

Savannah's lips closed over hers, swallowing her apology. This, right here, right now…this was what Eloise craved.

It had been twenty years since she'd kissed a girl, and all the feels were still there. Her body ignited, and she melted into the kiss. Revelling in the feel of Savannah's corset-covered body against her skin, she shuffled forward, unable to get close enough.

Without breaking the kiss, Savannah spun her around, cupped her backside, and hiked her up onto the massage table they'd sat on earlier. With her sight gone, her other senses were wide awake.

Every touch, every texture, every smell, was amplified tenfold. The anticipation of not knowing what was to come was intoxicating.

"Lift." When she felt a tug on her underwear, Eloise rocked her hips, letting Savannah lower them and pull them off.

It might've been her imagination, but she could've sworn her ears were so attuned she heard the lacy material hit the floor. A bang on the wall behind her made her jump.

"What was that?"

"Next room. Sorry." Savannah didn't sound very happy, and Eloise wondered whose head was going to roll.

"It's fine." The words came easily, but she had to admit, the din had taken her out of her head and muddied the picture she'd created in her mind of Savannah standing before her, staring at her lovingly.

It was her money and her scene, so she could dream.

The snap of a bottle cap had her back in the room in seconds. Cool gel circled her nipples before something plastic-like touched them.

"What's that?"

"Suction clamps. These rosy buds are far too delicious to be ignored."

"Thank you." Although Savannah had no way of knowing it, the compliment was one of the biggest ones she could've paid Eloise.

For years, she'd been teased relentlessly about her large nipples. *Is it cold out?* She could never escape that one, even in the summer. The only one who never paid any attention to her breasts was her ex.

The feel of the clamps tightening banished the unwanted thought.

"Beautiful," Savannah said. "How does that feel?"

"Exciting." The clamps tightened further, and a jolt of heat shot between Eloise's legs. "Oh, wow. That feels…amazing. Stingy."

"Wait until they come off." Savannah chuckled, a throaty sound rumbling in her chest.

Something cold pressed between Eloise's legs, making her jerk in surprise. "What's that?"

"So many questions. You'd make a terrible sub." There was that chuckle again. The playful one Eloise was sure would follow her home and invade her dreams.

A buzzing started, and she didn't have to ask what it was. She pictured Savannah standing between her legs, vibrator in the flat of her hand, pressed against Eloise's pubic mound.

"You truly are beautiful." She trailed her lips down Eloise's neck, igniting her skin. Her free hand brushed across Eloise's stomach, her arms, her shoulders, her breasts, around the clamps.

The vibrator changed tempo, driving her higher and higher.

Then it all stopped.

Mystified, Eloise wanted to stamp her feet in protest, but considering she was sitting on a massage table with her legs dangling over the side, she could do little more than harrumph.

"They say the sub has all the power, but I like to challenge that theory now and then."

"Not fair. You said I make a terrible sub, anyway."

"True. You've got fifteen minutes to change my mind."

The clamps came off, and she hissed out a breath. Blood rushed back, making her nipples throb in time to the pulse between her legs.

"Fourteen minutes."

Shit, what was she supposed to be doing? Ah, being a good submissive. She'd put that down as something she wanted to explore today, but she had a lot to learn and was thankful Savannah was playful in her approach.

That could change next time.

She kicked that idea out of her head. There wasn't going to be a next time. This was a one-off gift to herself to celebrate the new chapter of her life.

"Thirteen minutes."

Eloise pulled off the blindfold, scooted off the bed and dropped to her knees. The rug on the floor offered little comfort, but she didn't care.

With her hands clasped behind her back, she stared up at Savannah; the ceiling light bathed her in a blue, ethereal light. "Please may I taste you, Mistress?"

"You may."

Leaning forward, Eloise plucked at the hem of Savannah's miniskirt, pushing it up. Her gaze landed on a black G-string, and as sexy as it looked, she couldn't wait to move it aside and get her first taste.

"Did I give you permission to touch?"

"Yum." Was that a trick question? How else was she supposed to taste her? When Savannah continued to stare down at her, Eloise sat back on her haunches. "May I touch you?"

"You may."

Seriously! Taking her frustration out on Savannah's skirt, Eloise tugged on it, trying to pull it down instead of pushing it up. Maybe she wasn't as submissive as she thought.

Savannah clucked her tongue. "Terrible sub."

"You're right." She sighed. She'd had so many ideas about how today would go, and now that she was there, they'd all gone out the window. Not that there were any windows in the room that she could see.

"Come here." Savannah held out a hand, and Eloise took it, letting her pull her to her feet.

Tenderly, she tucked a lock of hair behind Eloise's ear. Melting into the touch, Eloise grabbed her hand and kissed her fingers.

"Lie back." Savannah pushed her back onto the massage table. "Close your eyes."

She obeyed. Something cool hit her centre, followed by the hot lick of a tongue that stole the breath from her lungs. She wanted to bolt upright and never move again at the same time.

When Savannah hooked her legs over her shoulders, lifting Eloise's backside off the white sheet, she had no other option but to stay put.

In what felt like seconds, she was on the edge, gasping and panting, hands gripping the edge of the table. She couldn't remember ever being so aroused…so fast. She was a throbbing mess. A ticking time bomb ready to explode. And wet. So wet.

Savannah stroked her thumb over Eloise's clit, and like a switch being flipped, she exploded into a mind-blowing orgasm. It was so intense, it felt like an out-of-body experience. Like it was happening to someone else because she didn't come that hard. Ever.

Until now.

She felt her legs being lowered, but she didn't want to wake up. Not just yet. She wanted to bask in the afterglow and the tiny aftershocks rippling through her body.

"You okay?" Savannah pulled Eloise to a sitting position, and she came crashing back to earth.

"Yeah." She braced herself to jump off the massage table.

"Uh-uh." Savannah shook her head. "Take your time."

"How much time?" She tried not to let the fact this was a business transaction intrude on the high she was riding.

"You're my last client today, so there's no hurry." Savannah offered Eloise a bottle of water.

"Thanks." She took it, unaware until that moment how thirsty she was.

And naked. And, oddly, she didn't feel self-conscious. Not even with her large nipples still on high beam. Hell, they were always on high beam. But today they were extra sensitive. She looked down at the imprints circling her areolae.

"The clamps," Savannah said. "You can take quite a bit. Aroused, you can probably take more."

"Aroused." Eloise laughed. "I just came like a trigger-happy virgin."

"I'm flattered." Her green eyes sparkled. "Sub, huh?"

"Sorry." She apologised again, feeling sheepish. "I was all over the place, wasn't I?"

"I like that. It's okay to plan, but it's also good to just go with the flow."

Savannah headed for the door. "I'll make sure the corridor is clear before you leave."

Alarm gripped her. "Why? Won't people having their nails done just think I've had a massage?"

"They will. But I'm talking about our *exclusive rooms*. Those clients don't get to see you, and you don't get to see them."

"Oh, right." That was reassuring, and she appreciated the efforts Libellule's went to, to protect their clients' identities. Imagine if someone she knew stepped out of the room opposite her.

Sure, they were there for the same reason and had no doubt been through the same rigorous screening as Eloise, but there were some things people didn't need to know. Friend, neighbour or otherwise.

Once dressed, she grabbed her shoes and purse off the chair in the corner. "Ready."

Inching the door open, Savannah peered out.

While her back was to Eloise, she took the opportunity to study her closely, committing the image to memory — sleeve of tattoos decorating one arm, long hair flowing down her back and over her corset, high heels that made her legs look amazing and the tantalising view of her garter belt peeking out from under her miniskirt.

"Okay, you're good to go. I'll walk with you."

She appreciated the offer. It would make her feel less like she was doing the walk of shame.

"Next time, you can use the back entrance. If you prefer."

"No offence, but there won't be a next time."

"Sure." Savannah's smile was self-assured. Perhaps she was used to women coming back for more. Or perhaps it didn't bother her either way.

Chapter 2

Right on four-thirty, the front door banged open and shut again, signalling Eloise's fifteen-year-old daughter was home. It'd taken some time to get used to not seeing Jack, her fourteen-year-old son daily, but Eloise consoled herself that at least she saw him every other weekend.

She had been over the moon when Mackenzie informed her she was going to play soccer this year. Since she'd been big enough to kick a ball, she'd loved the sport.

Then she'd quit, becoming a sullen teenager seemingly overnight. Having the bubbly Mackenzie back she'd missed for the past two years was the proverbial stamp on her divorce papers.

Mackenzie dropped her sports bag by the door and kicked off her sneakers. "Any sign of Ratbag?"

"No, sorry." It'd been almost a month since Mackenzie's cat went missing, and Eloise hoped she'd find her way home soon. "Hot drink?"

"Yes, please."

She heaped Milo into two mugs, inhaling the chocolatey aroma that rose up to greet her. With her ex no longer around to shoot her a disapproving look and tell her it would go straight to her thighs, she added another scoop for good measure.

"How was soccer practice?"

"Good. Our first game's in a couple of weeks."

"Where?" Eloise slid a mug across to Mackenzie and opened a packet of vanilla wine biscuits. No wine, but definitely more vanilla than her day.

Mackenzie eyed her curiously. "Are you okay?"

"Of course. Why wouldn't I be?"

"Because you look kind of spacey. Like you're smashed or something."

"Maybe I'm just happy." She'd been floating on cloud nine since her appointment at Libellule's. "I got these today." She tapped the papers sitting on the bench. "Your father and I are officially divorced."

Disdain twisted Mackenzie's pretty face. "I don't know why you didn't leave him sooner."

"Oh, sweetheart." She rounded the bench and pulled Mackenzie to her. "I'm so sorry." She would never forgive Anton for the damage he'd caused Mackenzie, or herself for the unwitting part she played in it.

Leaving him hadn't been easy, although it wasn't the leaving part that had been difficult—their marriage had been loveless for years—it was constantly second-guessing if staying was the right thing to do for her children. Turns out, it wasn't.

"He's still your father, and he loves you very much."

Mackenzie scoffed, pulling out of her embrace like a kid who no longer needed her mother to kiss her boo-boos. Sitting up straighter, her daughter dunked her biscuit for a second time. The soggy mess dropped off.

Harrumphing, she grinned, her sullen mood disappearing in a flash. "What's for tea?"

"Why don't we go out?" Thank goodness she didn't sign divorce papers every day. She'd done nothing but throw money around like confetti since she'd left her lawyer's office.

A pretty shitty analogy considering there was no confetti in sight. She was now a free woman. A woman who loved women. A woman who was getting ready to burst out of the proverbial closet.

"Can we go to that place on the lakefront?"

"Sure," Eloise said as if she knew exactly which restaurant Mackenzie was talking about, but it could be one of many along the waterfront.

***

The food was lovely. The company...not so much. "Could you put your phone down for five minutes?"

"Geez." Mackenzie tossed it on the table with a clatter.

"Want me to confiscate it?"

"No!" She snagged it with the tip of her finger and pulled it back towards her.

"Then drop the attitude." Mobile phones were still pretty scarce when Eloise was Mackenzie's age, but she still remembered what it was like to be fifteen. Even so, it was no excuse for insolence.

"Sorry. It's Bobby. She was messaging me about our coach."

"What about your coach?"

"She's a bitch."

"Language." Eloise forked some food into her mouth.

The chicken was so tender she barely had to chew, and the pasta sauce had just the right amount of garlic and herbs to make her taste buds ping. The meal was close to orgasmic. Her mind tried to drag her back to earlier in the day, but she fought against it, not wanting to give Mackenzie another excuse to tell her she looked wasted.

"What's so bad about your coach?"

"She's a hard-arse."

Eloise narrowed her eyes.

"What!" Mackenzie threw up her hands. "It's not a swear word. It's a body part."

"Just as well you're sitting on yours."

"What? Are you going to spank me as if I'm five?"

"If you keep acting like it…"

"God, I'm glad we're not on a date." Mackenzie's lips quirked in a smile.

Eloise returned it. She wanted to ask how she would feel about her dating a woman, but now wasn't the time. "Tell me more about soccer practice."

Mackenzie's phone vibrated on the table, drawing their gazes to it, but she left it where it was.

"Ms Sloane made us play this game called split the defenders, and then we had to do this drill called circle of cones."

"What's that?" It sounded straightforward, but Eloise wasn't up with all the lingo and didn't want to assume.

Another glance at her phone. "It's when you go clockwise and anticlockwise, using the inside and outside of your feet to avoid hitting the cones."

"So, she's a hard-arse because she put you to work?"

"Put me to work? My legs are killing me." She rubbed her thighs, full of theatrics. "I probably won't be able to walk in the morning."

It was wonderful to see the gleam in her eyes. "But you loved it."

"Yeah, but I don't want Dad to come and watch."

Hating that Anton had made Mackenzie feel self-conscious—it was hard enough being a teenager—Eloise reached across the table and squeezed her hand. "We don't have to tell him."

Mackenzie's phone vibrated again. Admitting defeat, Eloise nudged it her way. "Answer it."

While Mackenzie checked her phone, Eloise did the same. Two work emails that could wait until Monday and a text from Jack.

Can I stay at Logan's Saturday night?

Wonderful. It was their weekend together, and although Logan was a good kid, she'd hoped to have some one-on-one time with Jack. He'd been acting up at school, and she was hoping he might open up to her about what was going on.

Yeah, right. He was fourteen, discovering girls, and as closed-lipped as his father.

A bitter taste rose up the back of her throat. Grimacing, she swallowed it down and replied with a *yes*.

The smiley face she received in return buoyed her. She loved seeing her children happy. As a parent, that was all she'd ever wanted. As a woman, she needed more. Her kids would always be an important part of her life, but it was time to start putting her needs first.

Mackenzie glanced up from her phone, thumbs on the keypad. "Can I stay at Bobby's Saturday night?"

Great. Both kids were abandoning her for the weekend. "Will her parents be home?"

"I suppose so."

"Ask."

"No!" A few diners threw curious looks their way, then went back to eating. "Geez, Mum. I'm fifteen, almost sixteen."

"That's what worries me."

"I don't get you at times. You want me to grow up, but you treat me like a kid."

"It's my job to worry about you kids."

"It's your job to start enjoying life. Jack's not coming over, so you can…I don't know. Do what old people do at night."

"Hey." Eloise slapped her shoulder playfully. "How do you know he's not coming over?"

"Duh." She dangled her phone in the air, reminding Eloise that even though sister and brother no longer lived under the same roof, they were still close.

Thankfully, that was one thing the divorce hadn't changed.

Chapter 3

By four o'clock Saturday afternoon, Eloise had been to the supermarket, put the groceries away, cleaned the house, dropped Mackenzie at her mate's, and had the place to herself. She'd compromised with Jack that he could spend the night at Logan's on the condition that they spent Sunday together as a family.

If the weather was still cold, which it was forecasted to be, perhaps they could go to the thermal pools. But she could worry about that tomorrow.

Tonight, the house was hers, and she was going to make the most of it, starting with a soak in the bath. After lighting the fire, she put the plug in the tub and turned on the taps.

While it was still filling, she undressed and climbed in, sighing in bliss when wet heat enveloped her. Inhaling the aroma of rose water, she closed her eyes, allowing her mind to wander to the magical hour she'd spent at Libellule's.

The sense of euphoria making her want to burst was probably over the top, but it didn't change how she felt.

Free.

Liberated.

Being true to herself for the first time since she'd become sexually active was intoxicating. And she had Savannah to thank for that.

The thought alone conjured up one of many images she'd committed to memory. This time, it was one of Savannah's killer smile and alluring green eyes that made Eloise's stomach flutter and her toes tingle.

After towelling off, she slipped into a robe, poured a glass of wine and grabbed her iPad. Curled up on the sofa, fire burning, TV on for background noise, she logged into the app she hadn't told a soul about. Not her best friend, not her parents, and definitely not her children.

After jumping through a few cyber hoops, she connected. The site was exclusively for women looking for women and ranged from hook-ups to deep and meaningful relationships. Well, as deep and meaningful as you could get when meeting someone online.

No doubt that came after meeting in person, but for all the people Eloise had spoken to via instant messages, she hadn't felt a spark with anyone that made her want to meet in person.

That was partly—mostly—due to her own preferences. She wasn't opposed to the odd date, but she wasn't looking for love either. This was her time to shine. Time to do what made Eloise happy. And her afternoon with Savannah had done that.

Thoughts of her naivety made her cheeks burn. When she'd made her booking, requesting a dominant woman, she hadn't expected to be so far out of her league. But she didn't regret a second of it. Actually, that wasn't entirely true. She wished they'd had more time.

Get that idea out of your head. Once, remember?

Now that she was more equipped, she could start some new chats and see where it led.

A message alert sounded.

[Athena] Hey, how'd it go?

One word came to mind. *Amazing.* Followed by two more. *Thank you.*

She couldn't remember how she'd ended up talking to Athena in a private chat room, but one night, when Athena had mentioned she'd paid for sex, Eloise's interest was piqued.

At that moment, she knew it was what she wanted. It felt safer and cleaner, not to mention classier—blame that on *Pretty Woman*—to go to a professional establishment than hook up with someone she knew nothing about. Which was a total contradiction because she knew nothing about Savannah, other than her occupation, of course.

[Athena] Glad I could help. You going back?

[El699] I don't talk out of school.

[Athena] Touché. A smiling emoji followed, then a wink, then a tongue, drawing a smile out of Eloise.

It was fun—addictive even—being able to talk so casually about sex in a virtual room full of like-minded women. But keeping up with all the posts could also be exhausting.

[Athena] Did you sign an NDA?

[El699] Of course.

Signing a non-disclosure agreement had been the first thing she'd done. The next had been booking a doctor's appointment. It wasn't the first time she'd been through such an invasive round of tests for STIs, but this time her heart hadn't been shattered.

And just like she knew she would, Eloise had been given a clean bill of health. A clean bill that had resulted in the most mind-blowing orgasm she'd ever had. No oohing and ahhing in all the right places when she was actually drier than the Desert Road.

She'd been anything but dry at Libellule's. Quite the opposite. She'd been embarrassingly wet. But more than that, she'd been so all over the place, she'd run out of time to explore half the things she'd had in mind.

After thanking Athena again, a woman who she had no idea what she looked like or if that was even her real name, Eloise signed out of the app and hid the icon. Although she didn't often leave her iPad lying around, it couldn't hurt to play things safe. Jack probably wouldn't ask, but Mackenzie had her mother's inquisitive mind.

Peckish, Eloise popped a frozen pizza in the oven and poured herself another glass of wine. Back in the living room, she tossed a log on the fire and stirred the embers, watching them spark and catch light.

After closing the door on the firebox, she untied her robe and sat on the sheepskin rug. She'd never meditated, but she turned her palms up on her knees and closed her eyes, letting herself feel.

The sheepskin rug was soft as cotton wool. Voices on the television faded into background noise as a movie of her own making started playing in her head.

Naked in front of the fire, making out with a woman. Her hand wandered and slid under the waistband of her briefs. She explored the texture, running her fingers through the triangle of hair. And lower.

Soft. Swollen. Wet.

Her other hand gravitated from her leg and idly played with her breasts, pinching her nipples.

Beautiful.

The memory of Savannah's approving voice made her shiver.

Take your robe off. Imagining Savannah had issued the command, she slid the sleeves down her arms, letting it pool on the rug.

Lick me. She imagined pleasuring Savannah as she cupped her breasts, lifting them and squeezing her nipples with thumb and forefinger until the lines of pleasure and pain collided. The bite of the suction clamps came back to her, fuelling her arousal.

She lay back and parted her thighs, basking in how free she felt and revelling in the heat of the fire warming her naked flesh.

The oven timer dinged, and she almost leapt out of her skin.

"Fuck!" She lunged for her robe, feeling like she'd been caught masturbating by one of her kids. How embarrassing would that be? Thankfully, that was unlikely to happen.

Mackenzie always texted if her plans changed, and Jack didn't have a house key. He had no need for one; she couldn't risk it getting into the hands of her ex. He wasn't a violent guy by any stretch of the imagination, but he wasn't welcome in her home either.

Noticing only five minutes had passed since she'd put the oven timer on—that would teach her for setting it with only half a mind—she put it on for another ten minutes and returned to the living room.

Before she knew it, her iPad was back in her hands. It kept her fingers off more intimate places, but not her mind. The app was addictive. Telling herself she was only going to chat, she logged in.

Her self-talk lasted for as long as it took to see Domme101 online. They'd talked briefly before, but neither had mentioned meeting.

Some profiles said looks weren't important, that they loved women in all shapes and sizes, but she wouldn't meet anyone without swapping pics first. She wasn't a shallow person, but the cover was what drew the eye. The rest was what kept you coming back for more…or made you walk away.

[Domme101] Hey, how are you tonight?

[El699] Good, thanks. Just kicking back. Fire's going, pizza's warming, wine's chilled.

[Domme101] Is that an invite?

[El699] What would you do to me?

Holy hell. A week ago, she never would've been so bold. Waiting with bated breath, Eloise took a sip of wine, savouring the red notes.

[Domme101] Depends. Have you been a good girl?

[El699] Nope. I've been very naughty.

A part of her told her she should back off, but she couldn't. It felt far too good to finally be able to flirt with a woman instead of having to deny herself.

[Domme101] Then I would put you over my lap and spank you. Does that turn you on?

Should she be honest or lie? The thought of being flogged turned her on, but being turned over a knee didn't appeal to her. To each their own, but it was too much like what you'd do to an errant child, which Eloise supposed was the point. It just wasn't for her.

[El699] Not really, sorry.

[Domme101] Thanks for being honest. What do you like?

[El699] Not sure. I'm still finding my way.

[Domme101] Wanna meet sometime? Go out for a drink? It's easier to talk about these things in person.

[El699] I'm not looking for love.

[Domme101] Who said anything about love? Sex and love are two different things. I can separate the two, can you?

Intrigued, Eloise upped the ante. *Wanna swap pics?*

She expected to be met with a resounding no. Instead, her jaw almost hit the floor. Closing it, she picked up her wine glass and supped at the last drops.

Domme101, or whatever her name was, was stunning. Long, golden locks curled around a heart-shaped face, and she had the most amazing eyes — the windows to the soul.

[Domme101] Your turn.

[El699] How do I know it's you?

[Domme101] You don't. That's why we arrange to meet somewhere public, and you tell someone where you're going.

Yeah, right. She wouldn't be telling a soul. The only way anyone would know about this was if she was spotted when they met. So, she was doing this? She massaged her temples.

The oven timer dinged again, and she set her iPad aside. A slice of pizza to soak up some of the wine she'd been marinating herself in might help her think straight.

Huh! She wasn't straight, but she did need to think this through. Actually, there wasn't much to think about. If she said no, she would look like a tyre kicker — online to waste other people's time.

After dishing up a couple of slices of pizza, Eloise grabbed the open bottle of wine — one more wouldn't hurt — and returned to the living room.

There weren't many photos of her on her own, but surely she could find one where she looked half-decent. She scrolled through the gallery, her stomach sinking when her gaze landed on one of Mackenzie holding Ratbag, face buried in her fur.

Fur being the understatement. As a purebred Persian, she had it in spades. She'd been a present for Mackenzie's tenth birthday. When she went missing, they'd gone back to the flat they'd lived in before buying the house, but the new tenants said they hadn't seen her.

Distraught, they'd put ads online, at the SPCA, the vet clinic, on Facebook, and searched the streets, calling her name until their throats were raw and their hearts were heavy. The worst part was not knowing what had happened to her. Had she found a new home? Run away? Or worse, been hit by a car and crawled off to die?

A notification came in, saving her from falling further down that dark hole.

[Domme101] *Have I scared you off?* The ghost emoji that followed pulled a smile from Eloise.

She continued searching the meagre amount of photos on her iPad and finally settled on a picture taken last month. Even though winter was approaching, she looked like she'd just spent a day on the lake without a care in the world.

Needing a change, she'd put herself in the hands of her hairdresser. The result — golden-brown highlights threaded through her chocolate-brown hair.

[El699] *Perhaps you're the one who should be scared.* She attached the picture and hit send.

It was a self-deprecating comment, but just like she wasn't attracted to everyone, she didn't expect everyone to be attracted to her. Sure, it would hurt if she got a 'no thanks', but that was the reality of online dating. The trick was not to take it personally. Or so she told herself.

[Domme101] *Wanna fuck?*

Although amused, she also shuddered. It was too close to something her ex would say.

[El699] *You sure I'm not talking to a dude?*

[Domme101] *You brave enough to find out?* She added a date, time and location to meet.

The bar was a popular spot, and while that offered some comfort, it also increased the chances of being seen.

Eloise sent back a counter offer.

[El699] *Monday. Lunchtime. At the park.* It would feel less like a date. And to be honest, more exciting.

[Domme101] Are you sure you're *not a dude?*

Eloise smiled at her wit. Meeting at a park did sound like something a guy would suggest.

With any luck, their ease of conversation would continue in person. Although she wasn't looking for anything more than no-strings-attached fun, being able to communicate was paramount.

By the time they'd finalised meeting and Eloise signed out, her wine was empty and her pizza was cold. After stoking the fire, she blasted her pizza in the microwave and curled up to watch a movie.

Life didn't get much better than this. She loved her kids, but she also cherished the nights she had to herself. She had any number of places she could've gone, friends she could've called on, but she relished the peace.

The knowledge she had no one else to please but herself.

Chapter 4

When Domme101 — real name Dominique — messaged to cancel their meeting on Wednesday, Eloise was ready to write her off as a timewaster. That was the thing about online dating. It was easy to talk the talk, but fronting up was something entirely different.

But when she'd cited a family emergency and suggested another date, Eloise had given her the benefit of the doubt.

They'd agreed to meet at a small café in Acacia Bay. Being on the opposite side of the lake from the main shopping centre, it wasn't as populated and was safer than meeting at the park.

A silver car pulled to a stop, making Eloise's stomach flip. After a glance in the rear-view mirror, she stepped out of her car into an overcast day.

She fed the meter and pocketed her keys. Out of the corner of her eye, she saw Dominique doing the same.

She was thicker set than Eloise had expected...and shorter — things a face picture often didn't reveal — but she was far from disappointed. Dominique was hot. And it wasn't just her appearance. It was the way she held herself. Confident.

She glanced in Eloise's direction, a slow smile making an appearance.

When their eyes locked, her heart rate kicked up. It blew Eloise's mind that such a beautiful woman would even consider meeting her, let alone be looking at her like she was her next meal.

Dominique strode her way, knee-length coat swishing around her legs. "Hi. You must be Eloise."

"I am," Eloise said.

"And you're just as gorgeous as your photo." Dominique held out an elbow. "Shall we?"

Although that felt a little familiar, it was on par with her assertive online persona, so Eloise went with it, sliding her arm through the gap. As soon as they stepped inside, she reclaimed her arm.

The sweet smell of cinnamon buns and baked goods competed with the heady aroma of freshly ground coffee beans.

"What are you having?" Dominique asked, studying the blackboard above the counter.

"I think I'll have a flat white."

"My treat." Dominique stepped up to the counter. "One flat white and one Vienna."

It'd been a long time since Eloise had tried one of those, and although it'd been okay, the two shots of strong black espresso infused with whipped cream had been too rich for her.

The server rang up their order, and it finally hit Eloise that Dominique had offered to pay. A nice gesture, but she didn't want to feel indebted if things went bad. She couldn't see that happening, but one never knew.

"I don't mind paying for myself." Before she could retrieve her wallet, a hand stopped her.

Irritation prickled under her skin. Some of it was directed at Dominique, but most of it was at herself. Perhaps she needed to make it clearer that her desire to submit didn't mean she wanted to be ploughed over outside the bedroom, but standing at the counter with a young man waiting to take their money wasn't the place to get into that.

"I insist." Dominique's expression brooked no argument.

Not wanting to make a scene, Eloise acquiesced. They could clear that up once they were seated. Or she could just accept the offer and let it go.

And that was exactly what she did once they were seated — let it go. Dominique was easy to talk to, and she found herself relaxing more and more by the second.

She was also incredibly sexy, and her eyes were an unusual shade of blue. They seemed to alternate between dark blue and light grey, depending on how the light hit them.

"I know it's rude to ask, but how old are you?" Eloise asked as she ripped open a sugar sachet. It was a blunt question, but she was intrigued, and when it came to age, she was often way off the mark.

"You're right. It is rude," Dominique replied. "But I like you, so I'm going to tell you." She leaned in close, her breath fresh and minty. "Forty-five."

"No way. You don't look a day over thirty-five."

"Now I know you're lying." Dominique grabbed a lock of Eloise's hair and wound it around her finger, reeling her in like a fish. "You've officially earned your first punishment." She nipped Eloise's lip.

"Ow. That hurt." A lot, and she wasn't sure she liked it.

"Too much?" Dominique asked, her mistress persona slipping.

You think? Eloise glanced around the café, glad she didn't recognise anyone and thankful no one appeared to have noticed. "I prefer my fun behind closed doors."

"Me too. I was just testing the waters."

Eloise's mind flicked to the conversation she'd had with Savannah when they'd first met. She shouldn't be comparing the two, but at least Savannah had sat her down and discussed her desires and limits, which were pretty pitiful when it came down to it.

"Shouldn't we discuss how deep those waters run first?"

A smile pulled at Dominique's lips. "Wow, that was deep." She laughed. "Get it? Waters. Deep."

Letting her have that one, Eloise returned her grin. "Very clever."

"So, are you out?" Dominique asked.

Taken off guard by the question, Eloise scrambled for something to say. She hadn't known Dominique long enough to want to share her coming-out journey. If she couldn't trust her with that information, how was she supposed to trust her with her body?

Rather than give a direct answer, Eloise put the question back on Dominique. "Are you?"

She chortled like it was a ludicrous question. "I've been out since I was five." She dusted her fingers on her chest. "I'm a gold-star lesbian."

The announcement was like sandpaper scraping over a raw nerve, irritating the hell out of Eloise. It wasn't the first time she'd heard the term, and just like all the other times she'd heard the phrase so casually thrown around, it soured her stomach.

"Is that a badge you wear with pride?"

"You betcha."

"Have you ever stopped to think that could be hurtful to women coming out later in life?" *Women like me.* She kept that bit to herself.

"You mean all those bicurious women?"

A look of derision turned Dominique's once-attractive face into something Eloise wanted to recoil from. Although she knew she should just drop it, she tried to make Dominique see how hurtful those words could be to someone. Or maybe it was just her.

"I'm referring to all those women who weren't able to be true to themselves for whatever reason. Religion. Society. Peer pressure. Fear of disappointing their family."

"More fool them. You couldn't pay me enough to sleep with a dude. Not that I've ever been paid for sex." She looked physically ill. "That's a whole other level of ick."

That was it. This date was officially over.

She was hoping listening to her point of view would make Dominique more objective, but she was so focused on her gold star, anything Eloise said was lost on her.

Retrieving her phone from her handbag, Eloise made a show of staring at a non-existent text. "Shit. Sorry, I've got to go." She grabbed her jacket off the back of the chair.

"Something wrong?"

"Yep. My daughter needs me." She smiled an apology. "I'm really sorry about this."

"How old's your daughter?"

Glad she hadn't discussed her family, she pretended not to hear.

"Text me," Dominique called after her.

Not likely.

She flew out of the café as if her life was in danger, high heels clacking on the pavement as she dashed to her car. Firing the engine to life, she peeled out of the street, giving a perplexed-looking Dominique a little wave as she sped past the café.

Once she reached the intersection, she inhaled a breath. As she sat with her foot on the brake, hands gripping the steering wheel, she burst out laughing.

Talk about dramatic.

***

When she closed her eyes that night, it wasn't Dominique who plagued her dreams. It was Savannah. A sexy woman with midnight-black hair and a sleeve of tattoos.

Savannah who could teach her about the world of kink.

Savannah who was patient with her.

Savannah who predicted she would be back, and Eloise was about to prove her right. Ironically, she was going to spend her rainy-day money on something that would make her wet. She'd relived that hour over and over. What could another hour hurt?

Before she could back out, she logged on to make an appointment. By the time she logged off, she was both excited and disappointed. It hadn't occurred to her she might not be able to get an appointment that week. Her online contact had been quick to assure her there were other women available, but there was only one woman Eloise wanted to see.

It was going to be a long two weeks.

Chapter 5

Eloise flung her handbag over her shoulder and picked up her keys. The last week and a half had flown by, which meant it was only a few more days until she saw Savannah. Putting that out of her mind as best she could, she focused on her family.

Saturday morning sports were due to start, and both kids needed new boots. She could insist Anton pay for Jack's, but she didn't keep score when it came to making sure her kids had the right footwear for sports.

"Come on, you kids. Get in the car."

"I'm not a kid," Mackenzie grumbled as she grabbed her jacket.

"You're welcome to pay for your own."

"Love you, Mum." She made kissy sounds on her way out the door.

"Jack. Now!"

"Hang on. I just need to save my game."

"Five." She headed towards the living room, counting down each step. "Four. Three. Two…" She turned off the switch at the wall.

"What! That's mean." Sulking, Jack tossed his controller on the sofa. "Now I have to do it all over again."

"If you don't get in the car, you won't be playing your game for the rest of the weekend."

"Dad would—"

"Don't pull that card, mister." She pointed to the door. "Go."

She had no doubt Anton let Jack get away with murder, letting him do what he wanted, including gaming for as long as he liked, all in an attempt to come across as the good guy. But what he didn't realise was kids needed boundaries, and one day that might bite him in the arse.

By the time Eloise locked the house, Jack and Mackenzie were leaning against the car waiting for her. She pushed the key fob, and they all climbed in.

"Mum?" Jack said from the back seat.

She glanced at him in the rear-view mirror. He was a great-looking kid, with a tanned complexion, and wore his hair long on top and shaved around his ears.

"Yes?"

"Sorry for—"

"Being a dick," Mackenzie interrupted.

"Not fair. I don't call you a vagina."

"Okay, you two." Eloise put the car in gear. "Get it out of your system before we get to town."

"Jack-o-lantern."

"Kenzie kooties."

"Jack-in-the-box."

"Kenzie frenzy."

"Jack-arse."

"Okay. Enough!" Eloise snapped.

Mackenzie snickered. So did her brother.

After finding a park near Tongariro Domain, they all climbed out.

"Mum. There's Tim." Jack pointed to a kid bouncing on the in-ground trampoline at the nearby playground. "Can I go say hi?"

"Make it quick." She grabbed some change out of her purse and handed it to Mackenzie. "Be a love."

"Fine." She wandered down the street and stopped three car lengths away. "Rego?"

She should've thought of that. Staying where she was, Eloise called out the licence-plate number.

Mackenzie deposited the coins and ran over to Jack, dragging him away from his mate by his jacket.

"Can we get Macker's for lunch?" Jack asked as they crossed the road, ducking between traffic.

"Do you think Mum's made of money?" Mackenzie nudged him.

"No." He shook his head.

"We'll see," Eloise said.

It would probably cost her forty bucks for all three to have McDonald's for lunch, but that was a small price to pay considering the amount of money she was spending on treating herself to something very tasty.

And that something—someone—very tasty was heading in their direction. Like they were going to have a head-on any second.

Fuck. Panic welled up in Eloise. What the hell was she supposed to say? Not only to Savannah, but to her kids. Jack probably wouldn't care, but Mackenzie was bound to ask how they knew each other.

Maybe the smile was for someone else. Hoping like hell that was the case, Eloise glanced over her shoulder. There were other shoppers, but they were too far back for Savannah to be smiling at them, especially with a family of three blocking her line of sight.

"Hey, fancy seeing you!"

Under any other circumstances, the exuberant greeting would've been welcome, but Eloise was too stunned to speak. In the back of her mind, she'd known there was a possibility she would run into Savannah in public, which was why she'd made sure to shop at the opposite end of town from Libellule's.

Fat lot of good that had done. Just like not preparing herself for this very uncomfortable situation. Before she could regain her equilibrium, Mackenzie stunned her further.

"Hi, Ms Sloane. This is my mum."

"Nice to meet you." Savannah extended a hand, acting as professionally as Eloise would've expected, but rather than put her at ease, the contact made it worse. Those hands had been all over her. Inside her.

Fucking hell, El. Get your shit together.

Eloise released Savannah's hand as if she'd been burned. She felt like she had too. Her insides were on fire, and her brain was fried.

"That's Jack." Mackenzie pointed. "My brother. We're going shoe shopping."

"Boot shopping," Jack corrected.

"Oh, do you play soccer as well?" Savannah asked, looking down at him with a friendly smile.

"Nope. Rugby." He straightened. "I'm going to play for the All Blacks one day."

"Good for you, and if your sister keeps up the good work, she can play for the Football Ferns. Make your mum proud." There that panty-melting, steal-the-breath-from-your-lungs smile again.

Mackenzie kicked at the pavement. "I'm not that good."

"You can be."

"Aunty." Someone called out, drawing Savannah's attention over their shoulders, which wasn't hard given she had six inches on Eloise.

"Coming. Have a good day." She held Eloise's gaze for a split second, then dropped it to Mackenzie. "See you at practice." She stepped around them and was gone.

As tempting as it was to glance over her shoulder, Eloise didn't dare look back.

"Well, that was awkward," Mackenzie said as they started walking again.

Wasn't that the understatement of the year? Eloise was still trying to process what had just happened.

"Who was that?" Jack asked, oblivious to his mother's unease.

"My soccer coach." Mackenzie walked backwards, tugging on the sleeve of her jacket. "You should see her tattoos. They're bad-arse."

For the first time since laying eyes on Savannah, Eloise managed to find some humour in the situation. "So that's the hard-arse you were telling me about? Ms…" She trailed off, unable to recall the name.

"Yep. Ms Sloane. She's like, do this, do that. No, not like that."

"Harder. Faster," Jack joined in, unwittingly taking Eloise's mind to places it had no right going with her children standing beside her.

But who would've guessed? A soccer coach.

Shit! A thought slammed into her like the logging truck that whizzed by. It was as titillating as it was horrifying. Thanks to this new development, she would get a regular fix of Savannah at Mackenzie's soccer games. But how awkward would that be? Would she be able to look Savannah in the eyes and remain neutral? She could try, but her body would probably betray her.

"Mum?" Mackenzie tugged on her arm. "You spaced out again."

"I did not." She quickly recovered. "I was mentally checking my credit card balance."

"My old boots will last for the season if we don't have enough."

Maybe her quick recovery wasn't so fast after all.

"Mine won't," Jack said.

"That's because your father—"

Eloise shot Mackenzie a warning look.

"He's your father too," Jack said, looking small. Defeated and sad.

He didn't know the half of it, and he didn't need to. That was something both she and Mackenzie had agreed upon.

"Come on." Eloise stepped around a young couple loitering on the pavement. "Let's get our shopping over with so we can go to the golden arches."

***

Later that night, while the kids were busy, Eloise grabbed her iPad. Discovering Savannah was her daughter's soccer coach had changed things. She didn't know if she could go through with an appointment knowing that shortly after her hour was up with Savannah, Mackenzie would be seeing her. In a completely different capacity, of course, but it still felt wrong, somehow.

Deceptive.

Making sure the kids weren't paying her any attention, she opened her email and went straight to her booking confirmation. There was nothing to identify the exact nature of her appointment, and once again, she appreciated the measures Libellule's put in place to protect their clientele's privacy. It was comforting to know that if anyone logged in to her emails, they'd be none the wiser.

Hovering over the *Cancel Appointment* button, her gaze locked on one word — *non-refundable*.

Without sending a request for a cancellation, she logged out again. She'd paid good money for an appointment, and she'd be damned if she was going to pour it down the drain. With that decision made, her excitement was back in full force.

"What are you smiling about?" Mackenzie asked, leaning back in the beanbag, PlayStation controller in hand.

Trust her to notice, and Eloise wasn't giving an inch. "I'm just happy. Is that okay?"

Jack turned his head, gaze still on the game. "Better than being weird."

Chapter 6

Finally, the day of her appointment arrived. It was a typical autumn day — moderately warm — yet there was nothing typical about it.

Parking at the back of the business felt exciting. Naughty. And that sent a thrill through Eloise. For as long as she could remember, she'd done whatever she could to keep others happy, including marrying a man when she'd had the misfortune of falling pregnant at the age of nineteen.

She pushed the buzzer on the back door. No noise sounded, but she stepped back anyway. A minute later, it popped open, confirming what she'd suspected. A light had lit up inside, alerting someone to her presence.

An attractive woman with short, black hair and silver-rimmed glasses answered the door. "Hi. Can I help you?" Although her smile was welcoming, she was clearly on alert. When Eloise remained silent for too long, the woman prompted, "Password?"

Shit. She searched her brain for the word she'd been given. Her mind flicked to the doorknocker out front, and it came to her. "Dragonfly."

"Welcome to Libellule's. I'm Juliette." She stepped aside and motioned for Eloise to enter.

The familiar aroma of cinnamon and spice infused the air, and soft music played through unseen speakers.

"In here." Juliette stopped outside a door. "Savannah's ready for you."

Taking a deep breath, Eloise entered. The door clicked closed behind her, sealing her fate for a second time. Her gaze landed on Savannah, and her heart rate spiked.

She didn't have as much flesh on display as the first time they'd met, but she looked every bit as enticing. The black catsuit she wore showed off every delicious curve. With her long legs and striking green eyes, she reminded Eloise of a majestic panther.

"Nice to see you back."

It felt good to be back, but also weird after crossing paths in town. "Is this going to be awkward?"

"Only if you make it." Savannah aimed a remote at the light bulb, and it changed colour, bathing the room in reddish-pink hues.

"Don't you think we should talk about the fact you're my daughter's soccer coach?"

Savannah tilted her head, the right side of her mouth pulling into a smile. "Is that why you're here?"

"No." Eloise fiddled with her handbag.

"Good. I'll take that." She held out a hand. "Jacket and shoes too."

"Just like that?" Eloise peeled off her coat and toed off her high heels, obeying the order without conscious thought.

Savannah raked her eyes over Eloise's body, making her skin tingle. "You're stunning."

"Thank you," she replied shyly.

"If Mackenzie hadn't spotted me, I would've walked straight past and saved you from looking like you were going to have a coronary."

"Oh. Of course," Eloise said, feeling sheepish.

"Daughter, huh?"

"Yep."

"Married?"

"No!" Eloise softened her voice. "No."

It was a fair question. She could only imagine how many unfulfilled married women frequented the place. There were times she'd been tempted to break her marital vows — like the time she plucked up the courage to go to a gay bar — but her moral compass wouldn't let her go down that road.

Not even in spite. Actually, definitely not in spite. That would've been doing an injustice not only to herself but to the innocent party.

"I wouldn't judge you if you were."

She had no doubt about that. "I know. And my name's Eloise." She didn't know why she felt compelled to share that, but she was glad she did.

"Nice to meet you." Savannah placed a finger under Eloise's chin, gently lifting it as her lips parted. The kiss was purposeful, teasing and deliciously sensual. She tasted like strawberries and lust. The combination was intoxicating.

Moaning, Eloise melted against Savannah, basking in the feel of their bodies aligning. Savannah's tongue danced against Eloise's mouth, and she opened for her. Savannah's tongue slipped inside, velvety and warm.

By the time Savannah broke the kiss, Eloise was wet and her head was spinning. It took a minute for her vision to clear, but when it did, a picture on the wall caught her eye. If it'd been there last time, she hadn't noticed.

Red rope looped around the woman's neck and wove around her breasts, her waist and between her legs. But not just in circles, like she'd been abducted and bound.

There were four knots down the front of her body, each attached to another knot, and a formation of diamonds ran down her sternum.

"Beautiful, isn't she?" Savannah said.

She wasn't model beautiful, and she was all the more alluring for it. "Very."

"The Hishi Karada—rope dress—is one of my favourites."

"I don't get it, though." She'd read about rope bondage, but the woman's arms and legs were free. "She doesn't look very restrained."

"Here." Savannah retrieved a roll of red rope and handed it over. It was made from three strands twisted together and was surprisingly soft. "Jute and hemp are popular for rope bondage, but we use silk." She took the rope back and unfurled it, dangling the length between them. "I think you'd be surprised how restrained it makes you feel. Because that's what you enjoy, isn't it, Eloise? Being restrained?"

God, she loved the way her name rolled off Savannah's tongue. El-o-ease. Realising Savannah was waiting for a reply, she nodded.

She was met with a disapproving shake of the head. "Use your words."

"Yes, I like being restrained." The admission made her cheeks heat. She was a grown woman, for fuck's sake, with two kids and a household to run.

"You never need to feel embarrassed in here. This is a safe place where you can explore your desires until your heart's content." She ran the back of her fingers over Eloise's cheek. "Do you feel safe in here?"

"I do," Eloise said. "With you."

In the blink of an eye, Savannah was all business again. "Safe word?"

"Pickles."

"Good girl." She folded her arms, her appreciative gaze making Eloise's nipples tighten. "Strip."

The command fuelled her desire to please, to give over control, to forget about the outside world.

"Yes, Mistress." Eloise gripped the bottom of her shirt, pulling it over her head without bothering to undo the buttons. Next went her trousers, almost taking her stay-ups with them. Realising the error of her ways, she hiked her stockings back up.

And there she stood, hands behind her back, chest thrust forward, doing her best to resist the urge to cover her breasts when the glow of the pink light on her translucent bra made her nipples look bigger than big.

In seconds, Savannah was in her space, catsuit brushing her nipples. But she didn't go for Eloise's breasts.

She went straight for the kill, hand thrust between her legs. "Crotchless." A pleased smile lit up her eyes. "I'm glad you wore these because the happy knot goes right here." She captured Eloise's clit between two fingers, squeezing and releasing.

A pathetic whimper escaped Eloise, and her knees trembled. She wasn't afraid, though. The only thing she had to fear was wanting more.

"Eyes straight ahead."

Eloise obeyed, her gaze on the woman in the portrait. Would she look just as exquisite?

"If at any stage you want me to stop—"

"Pickles."

Eloise was rewarded with a sexy smile as Savannah folded the rope in half, tied a loop in the top and draped it around Eloise's neck before tying another knot in front. As she worked, she stood to the side of Eloise, constantly checking the position of the rope, both in front and behind her.

"I'm not in the lifestyle, nor have I ever professed to be, but I've attended some classes and know the basics." She paused, her alluring green eyes locked on Eloise. "Any breathing issues I should be aware of?"

"Only my heart galloping out of my chest."

She tied the second knot. "What about marks?"

"A mole on my butt cheek."

"I can see that." She swatted Eloise's backside. "But not what I meant."

Oh, fuck. Did she mean she wanted to mark her? "I'm not into biting."

"Good to know." She tied a third knot. "But again, not what I meant. If I pull the rope tight, it will likely leave marks for a while."

The very idea of that made her throb. She would have an exquisite reminder of today for hours after she left. Of course, the eroticism of the moment would stay with her for much longer. "Marks are fine. Rope marks," she clarified.

With a nod, Savannah knelt, putting herself at eye level with Eloise's centre. "Here, I can either split the rope and pull it between your legs…or tie a fifth knot." Even as she said it, she was already tying a knot, so it wasn't like Eloise had a choice.

Or did she?

If she used her safe word, Savannah would stop. But Eloise didn't want her to stop. Although nothing sexual had happened, a state of blissful serenity had come over her, and her mind was quiet. The need to overthink everything had disappeared.

Savannah tied the knot then pulled the two ends of rope between Eloise's legs and stood behind her, then she was back in front of her, adjusting the rope and repositioning the knots before stepping behind her again.

"This is called the happy knot for a reason." Savannah pulled on the rope from behind, sending a lick of heat up Eloise's spine when the knot between her legs put pressure on her clit.

The passage of time drifted from Eloise's grasp as she stood there, unmoving, her eyes tracking Savannah's every move until she was done.

She put two fingers under the ropes, pulling and testing. "Not too tight?"

"I don't think so." Why did she feel so spacey? It wasn't like her not to be able to give a definite reply.

"How do you feel?"

"Restrained." She sounded as baffled by that as she felt. "But my hands are free." She held them up and wiggled her fingers just to make sure.

"Maybe there is some submissive in you after all."

Right then, she was feeling blissfully submissive. It was something she couldn't explain if asked to. She felt dominated, yet Savannah hadn't issued a single command or tried to wield power over her.

"Face the far wall," Savannah instructed.

"Yes, Mistress." She spun around, relishing and cursing the knot between her legs. It felt exquisite, but there wasn't enough friction to get her off, only enough to make her throb.

"Safe word?"

"Pickles."

"Good girl." The flat of something smooth landed on her right butt cheek.

It had enough bite to make her lurch forward, but it also felt surprisingly good. Not as good as Savannah's hand running over the spot to soothe the burn.

"You really are delicious." She licked the shell of Eloise's ear. "Time to even things up." She delivered another blow. This one to her left butt cheek, soothing it immediately after. "Colour?"

"Pickles."

The paddle hit the floor, and Savannah spun her around, her eyes full of concern.

Realising what she'd said, Eloise cursed herself. "I mean green." She gave Savannah a coy smile. "Pickles are green."

"Oh." Tension left Savannah's shoulders. "Maybe you should pick another safe word."

Right then, she didn't feel like she needed one, but she was also aware Savannah was yet to test her limits. "Marmite."

"I prefer Vegemite." Savannah nudged her legs apart. "Let's play a game."

"I'm game." She bounced her eyebrows. "See what I did there?"

Before she could blink, Savannah had popped the front clasp on Eloise's bra and had both nipples trapped between thumb and forefinger. She squeezed and tugged, making Eloise rise up on her toes until they were eye-to-eye.

"You were saying?"

"Marmite."

Savannah released her grip, her expression all business. "Last time, because it suited me, I drove you higher and higher and pushed you over the edge."

God, had she ever. Eloise hadn't been able to stop thinking about that mind-blowing orgasm. It'd reinforced what she'd always known. She wasn't broken. Men just didn't do it for her.

"This time, because it suits me, you're going to get on your knees."

"Yes, Mistress." Eloise dropped to the floor, thankful for the thick carpet cushioning her knees.

With every movement, the happy knot stimulated her clit. Doing her best to ignore the ache between her legs, she clasped her hands on her lap. Slowly, she lifted her gaze, letting it travel over the glorious contours of Savannah's body until she met her eyes.

Staring down at her, Savannah lowered the zip on her catsuit far enough to reveal her breasts. They were full and round, her nipples as red as berries and just as succulent. She released the zipper tab and nodded once.

Picking up where she'd left off, Eloise pushed up on her knees and grabbed the zipper. She paused for long enough to admire Savannah's belly button piercing—a gold bar with a jade gemstone.

Unable to help herself, she placed a soft kiss on Savannah's stomach, loving it when her muscles flexed.

A tug on her hair made her yank her head back. "Did I give you permission to touch?"

"No, Mistress." She sat back.

"You may, but don't forget your place," Savannah said, her thighs parting as she spoke.

It wasn't until then that Eloise noticed the zip didn't end at the apex of her thighs like a pair of trousers—it ran between her legs. She parted the material, her gaze zeroing in on the thin strip of pubic hair as dark as the hair on Savannah's head.

A square packet landed at Eloise's feet.

A dental dam.

Excited anticipation surged through her veins, making her pulse race and her pussy throb as she ripped open the packet. The plastic sheet was so thin it was barely any barrier at all. She explored every inch of her, relishing in the feel of plump labia swollen with arousal. That was something you couldn't fake.

"Good girl." Savannah's fist tightened in her hair, pulling her closer as she rocked her hips.

Breathing in her arousal, Eloise braced a hand on Savannah's thighs, then sprang back.

"Permission to touch." Savannah's voice was firm, but a hint of playfulness underlined the words.

Relaxing her shoulders, she replaced her hand, loving the feel of Savannah's quads flexing beneath her catsuit and the heat radiating through the glossy fabric. As Savannah's movements grew more frantic, Eloise held her position, letting her take her own gratification. But it was both of their pleasure because Eloise had never been so turned on.

With a final thrust of her pelvis, Savannah emitted a guttural groan, her body quivering as she climaxed. Eventually, her body went limp, and she released Eloise's hair.

Chapter 7

"Up." Savannah held out a hand, and Eloise took it.

As soon as she was on her feet, Savannah claimed her mouth. Eloise snaked her tongue inside, drawing a low growl from deep within Savannah's chest.

Smiling to herself, she withdrew her tongue, but Savannah didn't break the kiss. She deepened it, cupping Eloise's backside, pulling her closer. They kissed for what felt like an eternity, and Eloise never wanted it to end.

But, of course, it did. "You're a good girl."

It'd been a long time since she'd been a little girl, but the praise made her glow. "Thank you, Mistress."

Studying her closely, Savannah ran her hands up and down Eloise's arms. "No numbness?"

"No." The reply was automatic, but she flexed her arms and legs to make sure. "They're good."

"What about here?" Savannah thrust a hand between her legs. "Sopping." She parted the ropes, exposing Eloise's centre. She pushed inside, drawing a moan from Eloise.

"Eyes on mine."

She popped them open, meeting Savannah's hungry gaze.

"Lie down."

"What? Here?" Eloise looked at the floor. The thick carpet looked comfortable enough, but still.

Arms crossed, Savannah tapped her foot. "Five, four, three…"

What would happen when she got to one? Would it all be over? Fuck that.

Eloise was on the floor in seconds. She hadn't known until then how many knots ran down her back, but she could feel two—or maybe it was three—around the middle of her spine and one higher, between her shoulder blades.

They didn't hurt, but she arched her back all the same, lowering it again when she realised she was thrusting her chest out.

"Uh-uh." Savannah tut-tutted, towering over her, nipple clamps in hand. "What did I say about not having to hide who you are in here?"

She didn't wait for a reply, and Eloise appreciated that because the bite of the clamps didn't give her time to dwell on anything negative.

"Colour?" Savannah asked as she leaned over and tightened the screws.

"Green." She held her breath, taking as much as she could because that line between pleasure and pain felt so damn good. When it started to really bite, she grimaced.

Reading her body language, Savannah backed off, and the pressure eased ever so slightly. "Okay?"

"Perfect."

"Good girl."

Moving to a tall cupboard in the corner, Savannah retrieved something and turned back to her, condom-covered magic wand in one hand, lube in the other.

"I don't think I'll need any lu—"

The stern look Savannah shot her was as good as any ball gag for silencing Eloise. Surprising the hell out of her, Savannah dribbled some lube on the inside of Eloise's arm.

"I think you missed." So much for the ball-gag theory.

When Savannah grabbed a crop and brought it down towards Eloise's clit, she scrambled back but not fast enough. It hit its intended target, but rather than hurt like she'd expected, it sent a jolt of lust swirling through her body.

"You liked that," Savannah stated, tossing aside the crop.

"Is that a punishment?" Eloise asked. "Not giving me more?" She would've liked to see how much she could take.

"Not at all. But we have limited time."

Way to bring her crashing back to earth. "Right. Business."

The look of disapproval—or was it disappointment?—that crossed Savannah's face was unexpected and confusing. It was as if she wanted Eloise to believe it was more than a business transaction, which was ridiculous...or part of the illusion. Yes, that must be it because there was no way she cared what Eloise thought.

Tissue in hand, Savannah wiped the lube off the inside of Eloise's arm. "This was a skin test before putting it on more...intimate places."

"Oh," was all Eloise could say.

Savannah had done nothing but look out for her well-being, and how had she repaid her? By feeling sorry for herself.

A dollop of lube landed on her clit, making her gasp. "Fuck."

Savannah gave her a wicked grin. "Cold?"

"Very." It felt like ice.

"Not for long." Positioning herself between Eloise's thighs, she ran her finger down the seam of Eloise's labia and parted her folds, spreading the gel. The feel of soft fingers on her labia and the texture of the rope running along the crease of her inner thighs made her throb with desire.

Things were heating up down there. Alarmingly so. "Um, it's getting hot."

"It's warming gel," Savannah said, using the pad of her fingers to massage Eloise's clit. "Tweak your nipples."

The command made her hyperaware of her bra dangling under her armpits and the nipple clamps sticking straight up. She flicked the tip of the metal clamps, moaning at the sensation that sparked from her breasts to her clit.

Then the magic wand was on her, vibrating with an intensity that bordered on too much and not enough. She didn't know whether to bear down to get more pressure or scoot back on the carpet so it wasn't so intense. Certain Savannah wouldn't let her do either, she closed her eyes, giving over control.

Savannah kept up the torment, vibrator on her clit, fingers inside.

Eloise's arousal built and built and built until she was aware of nothing but the pulsing between her legs and the burning need to climax.

A door banged, and Eloise didn't care. She was so aroused she doubted she would be able to stop if the building was on fire. Her entire body was poised to explode, and then it happened.

Writhing on the carpet, she tumbled head first into euphoria, a full-body orgasm making her cry out. "Fuck." She shoved her fist in her mouth to stop herself from crying out again as her body continued to pulse.

The vibrations between her legs ceased then Savannah was beside her. "You okay?"

"Perfect." She stared up at the ceiling, blinking against the bright, pink light.

"Sit up." Savannah eased her into a sitting position and sat behind her. The rope loosened, taking the pressure off between her legs.

She looked down. Even though the silk rope framed her pussy in a diamond, it hadn't escaped her explosive orgasm. "I think I ruined your rope."

"It's yours if you want it."

"Really?"

Savannah stood and pulled her to her feet as she continued to undo the knots. "Really. I don't use rope more than once unless I cover it." She held Eloise's gaze. "And it's not something I do often. I just took a chance you would like it. The way you lit up when you saw the picture confirmed my suspicion."

Touched, Eloise put a hand on Savannah's arm, imagining the tattoos beneath the catsuit. "Thank you. I'll treasure it along with the memory of today."

"Not coming back?"

"No." It was an expense she couldn't justify.

"See you in a couple of days."

"What?" She did up the front clasp on her bra and hiked up her stay-ups again. *Stupid fucking name for them.* "Didn't you hear me?"

"I did." She zipped up her catsuit. "Soccer."

"Oh, right." How had she forgotten that important detail? "Will that be awkward?"

Grinning, Savannah poured water into two plastic cups and handed one to Eloise before tipping back the other. "Why does it feel like we've had this conversation before?"

Because they had when Eloise first arrived, and she suspected she would receive the same reply.

Only if you make it.

She pulled on her trousers, wishing she'd had the foresight to put a clean pair of underwear in her handbag instead of having to drive home wearing her crotchless panties. They were wet and cold and incredibly uncomfortable.

Savannah smirked.

"What? Did I squirm or something?"

"Or something." She stepped closer, and Eloise's breath stalled in her chest. Was she going to kiss her? Again? Now that everything was over? Oh, God. She was.

It'd been a long time since she'd felt so desired, so wanted, and that was dangerous. Feeling like she was in a trance, she closed her eyes and let it happen. Savannah cupped her cheek and kissed her deeply. She tasted like sex and lust. She tasted like home.

What the fuck! Eloise's eyes popped open. "We can't do this."

She retrieved her jacket and purse from the chair in the corner.

"Wait." The alarm in Savannah's voice stopped her in her tracks. "You can't just go bowling out there. We have rules and protocols to follow."

"I know. Sorry." Eloise blew out a breath. "It's just…" Just what? That she was falling for someone she barely knew? Ridiculous. "I'm running late."

"Me too." Savannah glanced at her watch. "I have to be at the school soon, but if I'm late, the girls will warm up without me."

"Girls?" *Oh, right.* "I take it you're off to soccer practice?"

"I am." She glanced down at her catsuit. "Once I've showered and changed."

Fan-fuckin-tastic. Angry with herself, Eloise stared at the back of the door. "Can I go now?"

"Would you relax? It's not like I'm going to tell your daughter or anyone else for that matter. And I'm sorry for teasing, but you're adorable when you're riled up."

"My ex would disagree."

"Your ex is a shmuck."

She wouldn't get any argument out of Eloise, and that was a good thing because it was time to get going. She didn't regret opening this door, quite the opposite, but it was time to close it.

Chapter 8

Shortly after five, Mackenzie arrived home. She wore white shorts, and both those and her knees were covered in grass stains.

"I thought you were playing soccer, not rugby."

"Har-de-ha-ha," she said drolly, pecking Eloise on the cheek as she passed.

"Wow." She pressed a hand to her face. "What was that for?"

"Let's not make a big deal of it, okay?"

"Right. Sure. No prob." Turning, Eloise opened the oven and checked on the cottage pie she'd thrown together after showering. Putting Savannah out of her mind was easier said than done. The second she'd grabbed the Marmite to add half a teaspoon to the recipe, her mind had flicked to Libellule's.

Marmite. What a ridiculous safe word.

While Mackenzie was in the shower, Eloise checked the fire. Mesmerised, she stood there for longer than necessary, watching the logs catch and flames lick up the inside of the firebox. It was a mindless task that warmed her soul.

Hearing the shower turn off, she headed back to the kitchen and made two hot drinks. Mackenzie appeared, and she handed one over. "Tea won't be long."

"What are we having?"

"Cottage pie."

"Yum."

Together, they wandered into the living room. Eloise got a hit of Mackenzie's shampoo, and a sense of nostalgia washed over her. She'd loved being a mum. She still was, but watching her kids grow and blossom, cataloguing every milestone, had been the highlight of her life.

They'd made every slur she'd endured from her ex worth it. Maybe not worth it, but tolerable. They were just words, and with their combined income, they'd been able to give the kids far more than she would've been able to on her own.

She'd always planned to leave Anton once the kids left home, but his actions had driven that date forward. Shaking off thoughts of that horrible time, she looked to the person who'd been affected worst of all.

"How was practice?"

"Good. I got tripped up, though. Went down hard." Mackenzie rubbed her knees through her pyjama bottoms.

"By a teammate?"

"No." She gave Eloise a goofy smile. "By the stupid cones."

"Yikes. Embarrassing."

"Tell me about it."

"What did your coach say?" Why did asking about Savannah make her heart pound?

"Nothing."

"Really?"

"Yeah, she never makes any of us feel stupid. She just tells us to try again, and again, and again." She flopped her head back against the beanbag, arms dangling over the sides as if she was exhausted.

"Is she one of the teachers?" Eloise asked casually, hating herself for quizzing Mackenzie yet unable to stop herself. She had a burning desire to know more about Savannah, about the woman she was outside the parlour.

"Nope," Mackenzie said, half-distracted by her phone. "She coached the team last year. She's also my teammate's aunty."

"Bobby?"

"No." She shook her head. "Leilani."

"Pretty name."

"Yeah. And she's *super* pretty and has lots of nice things. But I feel sorry for her too."

"Why's that?" Eloise sat back, interest piqued.

"Because her mum is super old, and some of the kids at school snicker about it behind her back."

"How old?"

"I don't know. Sixty, maybe."

Eloise laughed. "That's not that old." She'd had an image of an eighty-year-old woman bent over a walker.

"Maybe not. But it's still gross."

"Gross how?" Eloise couldn't keep the amusement out of her voice.

Her mother was sixty and fit as a fiddle, but for some reason, teenagers thought that was ancient.

She couldn't blame them, though. There was a time when she thought forty was ancient. Now that she was approaching that age, it didn't feel old at all.

If anything, she was only just beginning to live her best life.

"Because," Mackenzie said, "that means her mother was still doing it when she was, like, your age."

"Cheeky bugger." The oven timer dinged, and Eloise stood. "Come on. You can set the table."

"Huh?" Mackenzie pushed out of the beanbag. "The table?"

"The coffee table," Eloise clarified.

Eating in front of the television was a terrible habit they'd fallen into since leaving Anton, but she couldn't bring herself to care enough to change it.

It was comfortable and warm, Mackenzie loved it, and she could watch the news while they ate.

***

Saturday arrived, bringing with it an overcast day. The streets were busy with families heading to the first sports games of the season—soccer, rugby, netball and hockey. As soon as Eloise found a park at the sports ground, Mackenzie was out of the car, grabbing her bag off the back seat and blowing out a breath.

"Nervous?"

"Shitting myself. I really want to win."

There was no point reprimanding her for being less than ladylike.

Eloise's stomach was in knots too. Both on behalf of her daughter and because she was anxious about seeing a certain raven-haired beauty.

"Hey, over here." A hand waving in the air caught her eye, and she busted out in a grin when she spotted Janelle.

They'd met at prenatal classes fifteen years ago and had been firm friends since. For years, they'd regularly got together for dinner parties with their group of friends, but since she'd left Anton, the group gatherings had become a thing of the past.

That was the funny thing about divorce. It separated more than just the couple. It divided friends. But she'd made her peace with that. What she'd gained—her sense of worth—was far greater than what she'd lost.

"Brr." Janelle rubbed her hands together. "It's colder than a witch's tit."

"Says the woman who loves skiing." Come June, the ski fields would be open, Mount Ruapehu would be covered in snow, and those who loved skiing could make the most of the longest ski season in Australasia.

"True, but you warm up fast when you're on the slopes." Janelle swung her hips as if she was navigating a slalom course. "Not that you'd know."

Eloise had only been skiing a couple of times, both times with Janelle's family, and even though Whakapapa Ski Field had the best beginners' ski and snowboard facility in New Zealand, she'd barely been able to stay on her feet.

Rather than help her, Anton had been his typical childish self, poking fun at her until the only thing warm had been her cheeks burning with embarrassment.

But that time was behind her now, and who knew? Maybe the new path she was on would take her to the top of Mt. Ruapehu, where she could glance out over the crystal blue waters of Lake Taupō.

"Maybe I'll join you this year."

"Really?" Janelle sounded both surprised and delighted.

"We'll see," Eloise said. She didn't want to make any false promises. "What field is Liam playing on?"

"Over there." Janelle pointed to her left.

Glancing sideways, Eloise spotted Liam and Grant, Janelle's husband. Then her heart tripped, and she almost stumbled.

There she was. Savannah. On the field adjacent to where Liam's game was getting ready to kick off. She wore a black tracksuit with white stripes down the arms and legs. Her hair was pulled back in a high ponytail, and her face was devoid of make-up. With the rapt attention of at least a dozen girls on her, she looked like a regular soccer mum, and she'd never looked more beautiful.

"Who are you gawking at?"

"No one." Eloise shook herself out of her trance. "I mean, Mackenzie. I want this to go well for her."

"She's back playing. That's the main thing."

"I know." Eloise looped her arm through Janelle's as they walked.

"Keep that up…people will think we're a couple."

Stopping in her tracks, Eloise met and held her friend's gaze. "Would that be so bad?"

"Um, yes. You're like a sister to me, and my husband would have something to say about that." They kept walking. "Admittedly, that would probably be to ask if he could join us."

"Gross."

"Exactly. So, yes, it would be bad. Very bad."

"You know that's not what I meant."

"I do. And that's why our arms are still linked. I couldn't give a rat's arse if people think we're a couple. Love is love."

Eloise pecked her on the cheek. "And that's why I love you."

"Naw." Janelle blinked her big blue eyes at Eloise. "Did we just have a moment?"

"I think we did."

Feeling a whole lot brighter, despite the nip in the air, Eloise stepped up to the sideline, joining all the other parents and caregivers anxiously waiting for the game to kick off.

Already in position as left full-back, Mackenzie was bouncing on her toes. She spotted Eloise and gave her a small wave. Eloise's nerves were back in full swing. They didn't necessarily need to win, but a good game would give Mackenzie the confidence boost she needed.

The teams were evenly matched for the first half of the game, scoring one goal each. By the second half, things were heating up, both teams wanting the goal that would give them the first win of the season.

One parent, pacing up and down the sideline opposite Eloise, was yelling at the ref and screaming at the team to get in there, to try harder. Why did parents do that? Suck the fun out of sports?

Janelle, who'd been watching Liam on the other field, appeared by her side. "Is Anton here?"

"No." Eloise shook her head.

"Who's the arsehole?"

She pointed to the dude ranting and raving, his face red as a radish. "It's that guy there."

"What a prick," Janelle said. "The poor girl probably won't come back."

"Perhaps she's used to it."

"Oh, fuck." She nudged Eloise. "Someone doesn't look happy." She leaned in closer. "Is that their coach?"

It absolutely was, and even though Savannah was moving with purpose, she looked as composed as ever. Unable to pull her gaze off the scene, Eloise watched in fascination and awe as Savannah tapped the guy on the shoulder.

She was tall enough that he didn't have to lean down to hear her, but he cupped his hand around his ear anyway, listening intently. He screwed his lips up as if thinking, nodded a few times, then held out a hand and they shook.

"Holy fucking shit." Janelle looked on in wonderment. "I think my ovaries just exploded. That woman's damn fine, and to put an arrogant fuck like that in his place…"

"You going to swap teams?"

"I don't know if my ovaries could take it."

"Damn." Eloise grinned. "Looks like I'll have to take one for the team."

"And that's why I love you." Janelle threw her words back at her. "Wanna grab a coffee after the game? Thaw out?"

"Are you saying I'm frigid?"

"No, honey. That was your ex." Eyes wide, Janelle slapped a hand over her mouth. "Sorry, that was uncalled for."

"Please don't apologise." Coming from anyone else, it would've been offensive, but surely fifteen years of friendship was long enough to be able to poke fun at each other. She'd been guilty of doing the same. "Besides, I had a good thawing last week."

"Shut the front door!" Janelle's eyes were like saucers. "Spill."

She'd already said too much, and she was supposed to be supporting Mackenzie. "Sorry, game to watch."

"Fine. You're off the hook for now."

Turning back to the game, Eloise's stomach jumped into her throat. She watched on tenterhooks as Mackenzie faced the opposition swooping in for a goal.

The girl sidestepped her, and Eloise's stomach went into freefall. But Mackenzie wasn't giving up. With a few skilled movements, she was back in front, the ball trapped between their feet in a stand-off.

Then the girl broke free, and the ball flew overhead. The entire park seemed to fall quiet as the goalie leapt into the air, deflecting it with both hands. The whistle sounded, and the referee called a draw.

Hoping Mackenzie wasn't too dejected, Eloise told Janelle she would see her soon and wandered around the field to where the girls had gathered around Savannah. Thankfully, the team was in great spirits.

She stood back, her heart singing as Savannah propped each and every one of them up, telling them how proud of them she was before adding she was going to work them to the bone at training on Tuesday.

Eloise did her best to fade into the background, but it wasn't easy, with Savannah being six foot tall. Their eyes met, and when Savannah smiled at her, Eloise's insides turned to mush.

It was odd to be surrounded by teenagers when she was the one crushing on the coach.

Spotting her, Mackenzie came running over. Eloise wanted to hug her but wouldn't dare in front of her friends in case it wasn't cool. "Hey. You did good."

"Could've done better." She bounced on her toes, looking hyped. "But it gave Leilani time to get in a better position to defend the goal."

Where had she heard that name before? Ah, that's right. Savannah's niece. "Which one is she?"

"Over there, by Ms Sloane."

It wasn't hard to tell which one she was. She was tall with sleek, black hair the same as her aunty. A middle-aged woman stood nearby. Even though her hair was grey, there was no mistaking her for Savannah's sister.

Although she was decades older, a story that intrigued Eloise, the woman had an elegance about her that made her look closer to fifty-five than Mackenzie's educated guess of sixty.

"Can Bobby come over?" Mackenzie asked as her best mate came sprinting their way. She was a lean teen with dirty-blonde hair she wore flicked to one side.

"Hi, Mrs Carter."

Although she knew it was a sign of respect, she wished Bobby would call her Eloise, but she'd reminded her so many times she'd given up. "Hi, Bobby. How are you?"

"Good, thanks."

"Can she?" Mackenzie asked again, smiling at her friend.

"Sure, but I'm meeting Janelle in town for coffee. She's probably already waiting for me, so get your gear and make it fast."

"Coach can drop us off," Bobby said.

Like fucking hell! Doing her best to remain calm, Eloise painted on a smile. "No, that's fine. I have to swing by home to get my coffee club card anyway."

Chapter 9

It was almost noon by the time Eloise dropped Mackenzie and Bobby at the house and made it back to town. When she rushed into the café, Janelle was already seated.

"Sorry. Kids."

"No problem. I ordered for you."

"Thank you." Eyeing up the two savoury tarts, she hung her jacket over the back of the chair and sat. "These look good."

"Which one would you like, tart?" Janelle's eyes crinkled with merriment. "Chicken and mushroom or spinach and blue cheese."

Gag. She could keep the blue cheese. "The chicken tart, please."

"Did you just call me a tart?"

"I believe that was you." Although it'd been said in jest, perhaps the title was fitting. Or maybe not. Did paying for sex mean she was promiscuous?

Janelle picked up her knife and fork and dug in, sighing in bliss as her lips closed around a mouthful.

"You look like you just came," Eloise teased.

"You should try it."

"What? Coming?"

"No," Janelle said around a mouthful. "The pie."

"I thought it was a tart."

"I would tell you to stop being such a smart-arse, but it's great to have you back." She put down her utensils and picked up her mug with both hands. "Now, tell me, what's gotten into you?"

"What do you mean? I'm just enjoying lunch with my bestie. Is that a crime?"

"No. But lying to me is." Her expression was thoughtful, and then she sprang forward in her seat, leaning across the table. "You've met someone, haven't you?"

Janelle was grinning widely, but Eloise couldn't return it. With her nerves jangling, she set her mug down before she spilled the contents.

From the day she'd left Anton, actually, long before that, she knew the day would arrive when she had to come out. Now that it was here, it was downright terrifying. She'd always envisioned it would be when she'd met someone, a woman, but she no longer felt she had to be in a relationship to come out.

In fact, it would be better to get that over with before she fell in love. Which gave her about…a decade. Okay, maybe not that long, but she wasn't looking for love right now. She was having too much fun exploring that part of her, an integral part of her, she'd suppressed for so many years.

"Why the frown line?" Janelle's expression was full of concern. "You know you can talk to me about anything, right?"

"I do." She did know that, and Janelle was the least judgemental person she knew, but it didn't make it any easier. Would their friendship change? Would Janelle stop hugging her, afraid the hugs suddenly meant more? She'd seen it happen to a school friend but that had been twenty years ago.

"You're right. I've met someone."

"Why so glum? Does he have ED?"

"No." Eloise laughed. "He doesn't have erectile dysfunction." She took a minute to gather her courage. "*She* doesn't have a penis." She emphasised the first word and whispered the last, which only made her statement sound all the more scandalous.

Scooting her chair back, Janelle rounded the table and draped herself around Eloise's neck. "That's wonderful."

She could've slapped her and Eloise would've been less surprised. She hadn't expected a look of horror, but she hadn't expected such a jubilant response either. When it sank in she was out, to her best friend anyway, and the world hadn't ended, relief flooded her.

"Thank you." She squeezed Janelle's arm. "You're the first person I've told."

"I'm not overly surprised."

Was she that transparent? Had Janelle seen her checking out other women? "Why?"

"Two years, El. Two years, and not even a hint of interest in dating." She reached over and squeezed Eloise's hand.

"I know you got badly burned, you and Mackenzie, but come on, a woman has needs." She sat back, arms folded. "Now, give me the deets."

A couple stood, and Eloise glanced in their direction. The gent helped the woman into her jacket. A breeze blew in as they blew out, and Eloise turned back to Janelle.

"I met a woman. She took care of my needs. End of story." She sat back, mirroring Janelle's posture.

"Wow. Go you. So you just bumped uglies and dumped her?"

"No!" Eloise snorted. "And mine's not so ugly."

"Not an image I need."

"Says the woman with exploding ovaries."

Janelle leaned forward in her seat. "Look me in the eye and tell me she didn't make your lady bits stand up and pay attention."

Damn, she couldn't do that. But she could try. "Nope, no effect."

"Don't bullshit a bullshitter. And stop deflecting. What was the lady of the hour's name?"

Although she'd heard the term before, and Janelle had no way of knowing she'd paid for sex, Eloise's stomach flipped all the same. She'd had more than an hour with her. She'd had two. And although that wasn't enough, it had to be.

"I can't tell you her name."

"Why not?"

"It's complicated."

"So's life."

That was true, and Eloise had a burning need to tell someone.

Someone she trusted, and she trusted Janelle beyond the shadow of a doubt. But first things first.

"Swear on your child's life you will never repeat this."

"You know you can trust me."

She sounded offended, and Eloise got it, but she had to be one hundred percent sure this wouldn't go any further. "Swear."

"I swear on Tyler's life—"

"Why did you pick Tyler? That's like playing favourites with your kids."

Her expression turned from sincere to exasperated. "Are you going to tell me or not? I'd recommend you do because you look like you're going to explode."

"Fine." Eloise leaned in close. "Speaking of exploding ovaries, the same happened to mine."

"On the soccer field?"

"No. Before that. Before I knew she was Mackenzie's coach."

Almost in slow motion, Janelle's jaw fell open. "Do you mean to say, you popped your lesbo cherry with that dark-haired Amazon?"

"If you weren't my best friend, I'd be utterly offended right now."

"If you weren't my best friend, I'd be rather pissed you haven't told me before now." She shook her head as if still unable to believe it. "What, where, how?"

"You know the *what* part. I had sex with Coach Sloane. Twice." She probably didn't need to add that.

It would've been easier to brush it off as a one-night stand. Something that happened once, never to happen again. But she'd gone back for more, hadn't she? Her body tingled at the memory.

"You're blushing."

"Am not."

"I can't tell you where." She could've lied and said at her place, or even that they'd got a motel, but she'd never lied to her best friend, and she wasn't about to start now.

"I wasn't asking for her address."

A waitress headed their way. Sometime during their conversation, the place had filled up and two couples were waiting for tables.

"I think we're about to be evicted." She grabbed her jacket off the back of the chair and stood.

Two minutes later, they were sitting on the park bench across the road from the café. A chilly breeze blew in off the lake and swirled around them. Seagulls circled above, looking for food scraps.

"So, where were we?" Janelle asked.

"At a lakeside café."

"I like this side of you," Janelle smiled warmly.

"What side?"

"The side that can't stop smiling. So, when are you seeing her again?"

"I'm not." The words alone were like a punch to the gut. Janelle opened her mouth to say something, but Eloise got in first. "Like I said, it's complicated."

"Is it? Or are you complicating it?"

"For various reasons, it will never happen again, so it doesn't even matter." It still hurt to say, but she was determined to move on. How did you date a sex worker? What did you talk about at night? *Hey, honey, how was your day? Did you get laid? How many times?*

"It does matter," Janelle said. "You're glowing. I bet if you walked up to the water's edge and stared into the lake, you'd see a giant fireball reflected back at you.

"I'm glowing because I'm finally out." She stood and twirled in a circle. "Free as a bird. I don't want to be tied down."

Chapter 10

As she pulled into the driveway, Eloise watched smoke billowing from the chimney, merging with the dark-grey sky. It'd taken weeks to teach Mackenzie how to light the fire, but she appeared to have finally mastered the art.

A ball of fluff darted across the yard, making Eloise's heart leap into her throat. *Ratbag?* Could it be? Dare she hope? Pulse racing, she was out of the car in seconds. She crouched, peering under the bushes.

A cat looked back at her, its eyes wide as saucers. Not Ratbag. "Hey, puss."

It took off, and she straightened, glad she hadn't alerted Mackenzie to the false alarm.

Inside, she shrugged out of her jacket, luxuriating in the heat that engulfed her. The only thing that ruined the moment was the blare of the television making her eardrums rattle. It was on the tip of her tongue to yell out to Mackenzie to turn it down, but the sweet sound of her laughter stopped her.

Surprised to see the living room blanketed in darkness, the curtains drawn in the middle of the day, Eloise tossed her bag on the kitchen table and headed that way. She stepped around the corner...and froze.

I'm cool. We're cool. Keep it together.

Mackenzie and Bobby were cosied up on the sofa, leaning against each other, hands entwined, blanket across their lap.

Spotting Eloise, Mackenzie grabbed the remote and hit pause. "Hi. I didn't hear the car."

Clearly.

"Hi, Mrs Carter." Bobby gave her a finger wave, all bright smiles and big brown eyes.

"Hi, girls. What are you watching?" Eloise asked, proud of how neutral she sounded.

It wasn't that she had an issue with them being a couple, but Mackenzie had never so much as hinted at being anything other than straight. Okay, she was guilty of the same, but it would've been nice if Mackenzie had talked to her before slapping it in her face.

Imagine if she'd just waltzed right in, holding Savannah's hand, no pre-warning. *No, not Savannah.* She shook the thought out of her head. Any woman's hand. She wouldn't dream of blindsiding Mackenzie like that. But Mackenzie was a teenager and they thought with their hormones, not their heads.

Although, Eloise's hormones had been talking for her lately, so maybe she should reserve her judgement.

"We're watching *Sex Education*," Mackenzie said.

"It's hilarious." Bobby grinned.

"Otis's mum reminds me of you." Mackenzie's lips quirked. "She's so embarrassing."

"Is that right?" Eloise could get on board with this. "Have you put your washing out? Your period pants?"

"Oh my God." Mackenzie stared in disbelief. "I can't believe you said that."

"Poke the bear." She opened the drapes. "Seriously, though. I'm about to put on a load of washing. If you've got any that needs doing, get it now."

Without replying, Mackenzie tossed the blanket off her lap and headed upstairs, looking like a teenager whose mother had just ruined her day. Smiling, Bobby stayed put. She was a pretty chilled kid.

Only, they weren't really kids, were they? And who knew exactly how much fun they'd been up to before Eloise arrived home. A thought that wouldn't have occurred to her a week ago.

Appearing outside the laundry, Mackenzie handed over a pair of jeans and a hoodie. "Here."

"Thanks." Eloise took them. "Where's Bobby?"

"Watching TV. Why?"

"Is there something you want to tell me?"

"No. At least, I don't think so."

"Are you two dating?"

"If you mean is she my girlfriend, then, yes."

"When were you going to tell me?"

"Geez. What's with all the questions?" Mackenzie was on the defensive, and it was hard to tell if she was being a typical teenager or lashing out because she felt trapped.

"It's the twenty-first century, you know. People don't come out anymore."

She put enough sass into the sentence to get under Eloise's skin. "That must be nice for some, but I don't believe that's the case for everyone, so drop the attitude."

"Sorry." She ditched the attitude and stared at the floor. "Dad will probably think he turned me gay."

You and me both.

Eloise could only imagine the shit show once the gossip mill made its way back to Anton. There was no doubt in her mind he would accuse Eloise of tarnishing their daughter. As if it was even possible to turn someone gay.

"Are you gay?"

"I don't think so. I like boys too."

"So you're bisexual?"

"Maybe." Mackenzie shrugged. "Does it matter?"

"Not to me." Eloise wrapped her in a hug. She loved this kid—both of her kids—beyond words. How anyone could abandon their child didn't even compute.

"There you are." Bobby appeared outside the laundry. She looked between them, worry in her eyes. "Is everything okay?"

"Yep." Mackenzie looped her arm through Bobby's. "I just came out"—she rolled her eyes like that wasn't even a thing—"and Mum's cool with it."

"Of course she is. Your mum's cool."

An hour later, she wasn't so cool.

"Can Bobby stay the night?" Mackenzie asked. "Her parents said it's okay with them if it's okay with you."

"Sure. I'll make up the spare room."

The look of outrage on Mackenzie's face wasn't entirely unexpected, but Eloise refused to budge.

"What? Why can't she sleep in my room?"

"You two are dating, right?"

"Exactly!" Mackenzie said as if that made everything all right.

But that was precisely why they wouldn't be sleeping together. If Jack asked the same question, he would be met with a resounding no, and she refused to set different boundaries for her children based on gender.

"I wouldn't let your brother have a girl sleep in his room."

"It's not like I can get pregnant."

"That's not the point." Eloise held her ground.

"I should go," Bobby muttered, looking uncomfortable.

"No, it's fine." Eloise blew out a breath. "You're welcome to stay, but you'll be sleeping in the spare room."

"I'm fine with that. My parents won't let Mackenzie sleep in my room either."

And that was exactly why Bobby was such a respectful kid—her parents set boundaries. Eloise narrowed her eyes at Mackenzie.

She shrugged. "You can't blame me for trying."

She had nothing to say to that because that was just like her daughter.

Chapter 11

Eloise had barely fired off eighty payslips with the push of a button when Taylor appeared in front of her desk.

"A custard square, please."

The office was open-plan with five workstations, numerous filing cabinets, light-brown walls and inspirational quotes that any one of the eighty staff liked to read whenever they needed to visit the office.

Once a week, the finance team took turns ducking out to buy morning tea. This week, it was Eloise's turn.

Martha appeared next. "Date scone for me."

She was a plump woman with a perpetual smile. Eloise had worked with her for five years and couldn't recall ever seeing her angry. She'd been a godsend during the separation, buoying Eloise when she could barely manage a smile.

How would they feel about her being gay? It wasn't like the topic had never been discussed at work, but it was different when one was amongst you.

God, what was she thinking? It wasn't like she was some kind of ghost walking amongst the living, and everyone would be shocked when they found out she was dead. It wasn't something she had to worry about right then, anyway.

She'd been quick to tell Janelle she wanted to be free as a bird, but that bird was yet to grow wings. She was hobbling along like a penguin. Although she was certain there were many lovely—and lonely—people looking for love online, since meeting Dominique, she'd gone off the idea. Or so she told herself. The truth was, Eloise lived for Saturday mornings.

Her heart always flipped when she spotted Savannah. Those couple of hours had left their mark, literally. She still had the rope tucked safely away in her bedside drawer. Those marks had faded, but the invisible marks, the ones that had affected her psyche, were taking longer to fade.

After taking the rest of the orders, Eloise tossed on her jacket and exited the building. A bitter wind whipped around her ankles and crept under the hem of her trouser suit.

As soon as she was in the car, she cranked up the heat. She wasn't sure why she bothered. The five-minute drive to town was barely long enough to warm the engine, let alone the interior. Still, it was a damn sight quicker than walking.

Inside, the aroma of coffee and baked goods permeated the air. A few diners were seated, but most customers were ducking in and out. She joined the queue and eyed up the cabinets, trying to decide what to have herself.

An Afghan biscuit? A slice of ginger crunch? Or maybe a Belgium biscuit.

"Eloise?"

Although the voice was tentative, Eloise would know it anywhere. Her body reacted the same way it always did: pulse racing, an intense throbbing between her legs.

Acting as casually as she could, Eloise slowly turned. If the food wasn't enough to make her mouth water, the sight before her was. Savannah wore faded blue jeans that sat low on her hips, a puffer jacket rested on the waistband, and her long hair was tucked under a beanie.

It was a total contrast to Savannah's persona at Libellule's and every bit as alluring. Hell, she could wear rags and she'd still be sexy. Her magnetism went deeper than the exterior.

"Savannah?" Eloise injected as much surprise as she could into that word, which wasn't hard to do. She was the last person she'd expected to see today. "What are you doing here?"

"Same as you, I suppose." She held up a bag with the café's logo. "I was hungry, and this place has the best sausage rolls in town."

So she was a savoury kind of girl. Spicy. Temptation on legs.

"Now that I've got you…" Savannah said.

Got her? An image of being thrown on the empty table in the corner of the café skidded through Eloise's mind.

"I was wondering if I could ask you a favour?"

A favour. Of her? What on earth did Eloise have to offer Savannah, other than her submission? And she wasn't even good at that. "Sure, you can ask. If I can help, I'd be happy to."

"Saturday, I'm planning on treating the team to an afternoon at the AC Baths. Problem is, I can't keep an eye on them all at once." She rocked on her heels.

The hint of vulnerability made Eloise want to know more about Savannah. To get to know her on a personal level. A scary thought. Enticing, but scary. She also needed to back the fuck up.

"Unless you have other plans, I was wondering if you would like to come along." Savannah lifted one shoulder. "You know, to help chaperone a group of teens."

"I'd love to." She didn't have anything planned. Hell, her kids and work were her life.

"Awesome." Savannah gave her a beaming smile and was gone, leaving Eloise staring after her.

Had fate put them in each other's path, or was Taupō just too damn small? That was twice now they'd bumped into each other. Who knew? Maybe they'd crossed paths before but the timing wasn't right, so they'd passed like ships in the night.

Hopefully, Mackenzie wouldn't mind her tagging along, playing chaperone. She'd never minded before, but she'd been much younger, and her mother hadn't been intimately acquainted with her coach. Not that she knew that.

"Next, please."

The woman behind the counter's voice snapped Eloise back to the reason she was standing in the middle of a busy café. Normally, she grumbled about having to leave the office when it was her turn to get morning tea, but today she was grateful.

Chapter 12

It was a close game, but a late goal secured their second win of the season. Witnessing fifteen teenagers high-fiving each other, all wearing matching grins, was epic. They could all quip as much as they liked that their coach was a hard-arse, but her training methods were paying off.

"Listen up," Savannah called out, trying to quieten down the hyped-up bunch. "Who's coming to the pools?"

Around ten girls bounced on their toes, hands in the air. "Me!" The others shook their heads no and waved bye to their teammates.

"Mackenzie, pick three girls to go with you and your mum, the rest of you are with me."

After a quick trip across Taupō from the sports ground to the hot pools, they all bounced back out of the car. With her ears ringing—who knew teenagers could be so loud?—Eloise climbed out, glad for the brief reprieve.

The scent of chlorine and excitement swirled around her. So did her daughter, circling her like a shark. "Don't embarrass me."

"Just for that, I will. I'm going to pop my boob out and flash—"

"Don't you dare!" Mackenzie shot her a mortified glare.

Eloise didn't give an inch. Let her keep guessing.

Bobby sidled up next to Mackenzie, looping their arms together. "What's up?"

"Mum said she's going to flash her boobs."

"Ew, nasty." Her smile was cheeky.

The side door on Savannah's van slid open, and five girls piled out, followed by Leilani and Savannah. As they walked towards the entrance, the loud chatter started up again.

"First one inside pays," Savannah called out.

The teens slowed their pace, waiting by the door for Savannah. Eloise hung back, admiring the way Savannah interacted with them as if she cared about every one of them. Did she have kids?

"Coming?" Savannah asked, holding the door open for Eloise.

I'd love to. Keeping those words to herself, Eloise smiled her thanks as she stepped inside. The smell of chlorine was thicker in here, and people were in different degrees of dress. Some scurried in and out of changing rooms, others waited to be served.

"Ten teenagers and…" Savannah looked at Eloise, waiting for an answer. She appreciated she hadn't assumed she was swimming even though she had a bag flung over her shoulder.

"She's just spectating," Mackenzie answered for her.

"Two adults," Eloise confirmed, tugging on the lapels of her jacket as if she was about to flash some skin.

Lips pursed, Mackenzie turned, dragging a grinning Bobby with her to the changing rooms.

"What was that about?" Savannah stood beside her, watching them go.

"I told Mackenzie I was going to flash my boobs."

"I can't wait."

Eloise gave her a sidelong look. "It was a joke."

"Pity. Come on. Let's get changed."

Standing side by side, Eloise kept her gaze straight ahead as she ditched her winter clothes and slipped into her togs. Why did this feel more intimate than being stripped bare and ravished at the parlour? She felt like she was fifteen again, trying not to steal glances at her high school crush.

Straightening, she adjusted the shoulder straps, making sure everything was tucked away, then wrapped a towel under her arms and knotted it between her breasts.

"Okay, ladies. Listen up," Savannah said. "Janine. Casey. You too." The area around them fell silent, all eyes on their coach. "Stick close. Look out for each other. No dive-bombs—"

"Or belly flops," Leilani said.

"Or belly flops." Savannah held out a hand. "Stash your phones or give them to me."

Eloise looked at Mackenzie but didn't single her out. She was old enough to make sure her phone was locked away or hand it over.

The group headed outside. The AC Baths included an outdoor leisure pool, two hydro-slides, four private mineral pools, a sauna and a café.

The pools were thermally heated, and numerous families were making the most of the facilities. Ten girls dropped their towels and took off running.

"Hey," Savannah called after them. "No running."

"Oops." Laughing, they slowed, walking as fast as they could, butts swaying, hips bumping as they rushed towards the hydro-slides.

Savannah tossed her towel on the pile. "Coming in?"

"I might just stay here. Keep an eye on things." The only thing she was keeping an eye on was Savannah's tall, lean body. She wanted to lick her in long, slow sweeps, savouring her like an ice cream.

She shivered. It was too freaking cold to be thinking about ice cream or standing there fantasising about devouring her daughter's soccer coach.

"Who's going to look out for the girls?" Her argument was weak. They could see them from the pool, and Eloise had spotted at least five lifeguards, which made her wonder why Savannah had asked her along. "You didn't really need me to play chaperone, did you?"

"Sure I did. My van only takes six passengers."

"Oh, so you're using me for my car?"

That earned her a grin, and she mentally high-fived herself, elated the joke hadn't fallen flat.

"You got me." Savannah tugged on Eloise's towel. The knot popped free, and time froze. Their eyes locked, cool air igniting between them.

"Wahoo!"

Recognising Mackenzie's voice, Eloise turned in time to see her daughter come rocketing out of the hydro-slide. Bobby was next, almost landing on top of her.

"Did you know they were dating?" Eloise asked.

"Not officially, but I'm not surprised." Savannah headed down the ramp into the pool, and Eloise took a moment to admire the swing of her hips, the way her bathing suit hugged her curves, the sleeve of tattoos decorating her left arm, and her long hair flowing down her back.

Someone bumped into her, and Eloise apologised for holding up the queue.

With half as much grace as Savannah, she tiptoed in, wincing at the needle-like pain when warm water washed over her cold toes. Once her body adjusted to the temperature, she sighed in bliss, sinking down until the water was swishing around her neck, her back against the pool wall.

Although it was supposed to be safe to put your head under, she wasn't a fan. She'd been dunked too many times by Anton to find anything appealing about it. Besides, she didn't want to ruin her make-up.

Yep, she was that person who wore make-up to go swimming. It hadn't been a conscious choice, she simply hadn't had time to remove it between leaving the soccer fields and arriving at the AC Baths.

Snaking an arm out of the water, Savannah waved to someone.

Eloise turned, waving as well when Leilani hoisted herself out of the pool and headed back up the stairs to the slides.

"You seem close to your niece."

"She's my world."

That was a strong statement. Something Eloise would say about her own children, but not about her nieces or nephews. Maybe Savannah lived with her sister and had been there, living in the same house, since Leilani was a baby.

It was still hard to reconcile that the grey-haired woman who turned up at every game was Savannah's sister. She had to be at least twenty years older. Come to think of it, she wasn't there this morning.

A pool noodle floated their way, and Savannah pushed it back to the kid chasing after it.

"I didn't see your sister today. Is she okay?"

"My sister died when I was eighteen."

Oh, shit. Eloise put a hand on Savannah's arm, wondering if the tattoos had any significance. "I'm so sorry." She meant it from the bottom of her heart.

She couldn't imagine the pain of losing a sibling. It wasn't often she saw her two younger sisters, but if anything happened to either of them, she would be devastated.

"It's okay. I've had a long time to process."

"How long?" she asked as gently as she could.

Savannah grinned, and although that smile could melt the pants off Eloise, she felt like she was missing something.

"Sixteen years. I'm thirty-four."

That hadn't been what she was going for, and it was also younger than Eloise would've thought. Not because Savannah looked older, but she had a maturity that belied her age.

"Enough about me. Your turn."

It felt wrong to dismiss her loss so quickly, but Eloise knew when to back off. "Two sisters. One's thirty, the other is thirty-three."

"And you're thirty-six."

"Good guess."

"I was going by the rule of threes. The other option was twenty-seven."

"Are you saying I don't look youthful?" Eloise asked, a hint of amusement in her voice.

"I was hoping like hell you weren't eleven when you had Mackenzie."

"True." She'd done the math quicker than Eloise.

One of the team members came rushing over and crouched behind them on the pool's edge. "Coach, is it okay if we go to the big pool?"

"It's raining."

It was? Eloise looked to the other side of the pool they were lounging in. An arched roof covered half of it, and on the other side, drops of rain danced across the surface.

"So? We're already wet." Janine shook her body like a dog, hair flying around her face.

"Off you go, then. Keep an eye on each other."

"Do you want to get out?" Eloise asked once they were alone again.

"Not really. I'm rather comfortable here."

A surge of water made Eloise tilt sideways. "Sorry." Reluctantly, she peeled her arm off Savannah's.

"Why so jumpy?"

"I don't know. It feels weird, sitting here talking so casually when we've been…"

"Been what?" Savannah lifted an eyebrow, an amused smile tugging at her lips.

"Intimate." Heat rose up Eloise's neck, and she hoped the steam rising off the water hid some of her blush.

"Don't you normally talk to people you've had sex with?"

Flustered, she blew out a breath. "Of course."

"It's not so weird then, is it?"

She was right. There was no need to make such a big deal out of this, but she couldn't help it. Savannah's close proximity made it hard to think about anything other than the brush of her hand against Eloise's leg and the mind-blowing orgasms they'd shared.

She cleared her throat and changed the topic. "So, we have something in common."

"What's that?"

"We both have two sisters."

"No." Savannah shook her head, the ends of her black hair floating on top of the water like an oil slick.

What a horrible analogy. Fancy comparing something so beautiful to something so tragic.

"Leilani's mum. Isn't she your sister?" If Leilani was Savannah's niece, Leilani's mother had to be her sister, right?

"She's my mum."

Confused, Eloise stared out at the dark-grey sky, trying to fit the pieces together, but nothing was aligning. "What am I missing?"

"Leilani was a baby when my sister and her partner were killed in a car accident. Mum adopted her. So I guess you could say I have a little sis. If I wasn't such a waste of space when she was a toddler, she might've called me that."

"I can't imagine you being a waste of space."

"Oh, believe me, I've done many things I'm not proud of." She nudged Eloise. "Tell me about you."

Catching on to Savannah's penchant for turning the tables when she was feeling uncomfortable, Eloise played along. "I'm the proverbial good girl. Well, I was until I got myself pregnant at the age of nineteen."

"Impressive." She lifted an eyebrow. "You did that all by yourself? Most lesbians who want to be a mother would envy you."

Eloise snorted. "Not quite what I meant. And most lesbians would tell me I got what I deserved."

"Why?" Savannah linked their hands under the water, genuine concern in her gaze. "What did you deserve? To have two children you're proud of?"

Eloise loved how Savannah could turn something she was going to dwell on into something positive. "You're right. I'm lucky. What about you? Any kids?"

She shook her head. "God, no. I don't have time. What, with working two jobs, three if you count coaching, and taking care of Mum and Leilani."

It sounded to Eloise like she wasn't the only one who put others before herself, but she didn't go there. They were supposed to be having fun, not bringing the mood as low as the dark clouds.

"Two jobs?" Eloise asked.

"A good portion of my day is spent on beauty therapy. So, yeah, I call it two jobs. One Mum knows about, the other…" She shrugged, no further explanation required. "What about Eloise? What does Eloise do for a job?"

"I'm a pay clerk."

"Number cruncher."

"Yes and no." Half of her job was keeping up with legislation for shift workers, tax rates, public holidays, days in lieu, ordinary pay, overtime rates, yadda, yadda, yadda. "Like you, a good chunk of my job isn't actually processing wages. It's all the other fun stuff."

"I like the fun stuff." Savannah bounced her eyebrows.

Right on cue, a plastic ball bobbed across the water, heading their way. When Savannah spotted the girl looking for it, she lobbed it through the air.

"Speaking of fun stuff," Eloise said. "When did you start coaching?"

"Ten years ago. Leilani was six. Her coach was away, and I subbed for her."

"Subbed, huh?" Eloise laughed.

"How did I not see that coming?" She bumped Eloise's shoulder, sending a surge of water up her neck. "I enjoyed it, and it was a great way to give back to the community. I enrolled in an online course, attended some one-on-one training, and as the saying goes, the rest is history."

"I think that's admirable." There were so many layers to her, the more Eloise unearthed the more she wanted to know. But she also didn't want to pry. Savannah would share what she wanted, when she wanted, and Eloise would soak it up like a sponge.

"Do you think we should gather up the girls before it starts bucketing down?"

"Yeah, we probably should."

Straightening, Eloise pushed to her feet, propelling her upper body out of the water.

Fucking hell. It was freezing. Goosebumps erupted on her flesh as she tore over to the outdoor locker and grabbed her beach towel. They were hardly at the beach, but it was the biggest towel she owned, and it wrapped around her like a blanket.

Nearby, teens were frolicking and laughing, climbing in and out of the pools as if it was summer. At what age did you start feeling the cold more acutely? Eloise couldn't remember a time she hadn't felt the cold.

Head tilted to one side, Savannah dried the ends of her hair. "Fancy grabbing a drink tonight?"

The invitation took Eloise by surprise. Savannah had asked her out. For a drink. Together. What a ditz.

Anyone would think she was sixteen all over again.

"Sure. Sounds good." Her calm reply belied the swirl of emotions making her want to burst out of her skin.

She'd never been this excited about 'grabbing a drink' with someone. Probably because she'd never been invited out by a beautiful woman. Domme101 didn't count.

"Full disclosure. I'm not a gold-star lesbian."

Savannah wrapped her towel around her waist and pulled on a sweatshirt, covering all that delicious flesh. "Is that a thing?"

Of course she didn't care about such trivia. Feeling stupid, Eloise shrugged. "I don't know. I've just heard the term tossed about."

"You could be pan or bisexual. I don't really care. I'm attracted to you as a person."

Savannah was attracted to her. Why did that make her giddy with excitement?

"What time are you free tonight?"

"Anytime."

Savannah chuckled. "You're adorable." She reached out as if she was going to brush a lock of wet hair off Eloise's face, then thought better of it.

Relieved, Eloise blew out a breath. She welcomed the intimate touch, but she didn't want to blindside Mackenzie like that. Not again. She was still dealing with the aftermath of her father's actions.

"So, if I said ten o'clock, that would be okay?"

Seeing her point, Eloise tried again. "What about seven?"

"Seven works for me."

Somehow, they managed to exchange numbers before a horde of ten girls came stampeding their way. When Mackenzie asked if she could stay at Bobby's for the night, it was a no-brainer.

She would see how tonight went, and then think about coming out to her daughter. She wasn't sure what would be harder—telling her she was gay or telling her who she was seeing.

Mackenzie's soccer coach.

The hard-arse. The hard-arse with glorious tattoos that Eloise still hadn't had a chance to ask about. Tonight, though, she hoped to change that.

Chapter 13

After spending way too long agonising over what to wear, Eloise finally settled on a pair of dark-blue jeans and paired them with ankle boots and her favourite top—a light-brown, polo-neck jersey with lace knit detail on the front. The blend of merino wool, possum fur and silk fibres felt glorious against her skin.

Not as delectable as Savannah's hands all over her, but that wasn't what tonight was about. She'd given Eloise a brief glimpse of herself, and Eloise wanted more. What had taken her sister from her life?

In her haste to get Mackenzie out the door, she'd forgotten to enlighten her that Leilani's mum was actually her grandmother. A woman who'd likely put her life on hold to raise her granddaughter.

Turning her attention back to the night ahead, Eloise appraised herself in the mirror. She fluffed up her hair, surprised how much it'd grown in the few short weeks since she'd had golden highlights threaded through the brown. A lick of gold eyeshadow brought out the flecks in her eyes, and a coat of rose lipstick completed her make-up regime.

Happy with her appearance, she spritzed on some perfume and practically floated down the stairs. In all her thirty-six years, she'd never been so excited about going on a date. Or perhaps it wasn't a date. She didn't know, but one thing was for sure — she was fizzing with excitement.

***

With winter closing in fast, it was long dark by the time she pulled to a stop outside the bar at seven. Street lights lit up the night and people walked with hands stuffed in pockets to ward off the chill.

After locking the car, she clutched her collar and stepped up onto the pavement. By the time she lifted her gaze, Savannah was standing in front of her. Where the hell had she come from?

"You're like a ghost."

"Believe me, I'm very much alive." She raked an appreciative gaze over Eloise. "You look beautiful."

"Thank you. So do you." Savannah's hair blended seamlessly with the dark night and her leather jacket.

Her green eyes were as alluring as ever. Eloise could stare into them for hours. There was a warmth there. A deep sense of caring when you looked closely.

She held open the door, letting Eloise enter first, the same as she'd done at the pools.

"Chivalrous and sexy."

"Careful," Savannah said. "I might start to think this is a date."

"Is it? I mean are you allowed to…" She trailed off when they reached the bar.

A bartender appeared before them. "What will it be, ladies?"

"A paddle for me," Savannah said, a flicker of amusement shining in her eyes.

Of course, Eloise's brain flicked to the implements hanging on the walls at Libellule's, but she wasn't gullible enough to think she was talking about that kind of paddle. "What's that?"

"Do you drink beer?"

It wasn't her first choice, but she didn't mind it either. Plus it was lower in alcohol than wine, which wasn't a bad thing when she was driving. "I've been known to."

"Two paddles," Savannah said to the bartender.

A few minutes later, they both picked up their paddles—a long, rectangular piece of wood with four holes that held small glasses with an assortment of tap beers. A more fitting name would probably be a sample tray, but it wasn't really a tray. More like an oar. A paddle. *Doh.* The penny dropped.

Seated, Savannah sipped on a dark beer and smacked her lips together. "Damn, that's good." She set the glass down on the small, round table between them. "You were saying. Am I allowed to…"

It took Eloise a minute to recall what she'd been saying. When it came to her, she considered pretending she'd forgotten, but she was certain Savannah would see right through her, and she didn't want to lie.

Buying herself some time, Eloise picked up one of the glasses of beer, savouring the subtle notes of espresso and dark chocolate.

"Are you allowed to date clients? Not that I'm a client anymore. And before you ask, I'm not trying to get the cow for free."

Savannah chuckled, not the least bit offended about being referred to as a cow. "Don't you mean the milk?"

"Maybe." She had a feeling she'd ballsed that up, but she couldn't remember how the saying went.

"To answer your question, that depends who you ask. There are no hard and fast rules about not dating our clients…or ex-clients. But a couple of the girls, one in particular, would advise strongly against it."

"Why's that?"

"She got burnt. Badly."

"What happened?"

"Not my story to tell."

With nothing to say to that, Eloise took another sip of beer. Now that she thought about it, Savannah was probably bound by a similar non-disclosure agreement as Eloise.

"My boss is engaged to a woman who used to be a client. And the business owner, who's a silent partner, married our previous cleaner."

Perhaps it was okay to talk about, after all. Then again, Savannah hadn't given any names, and Eloise wouldn't know who her boss was if she fell over her.

"So it does happen?"

"On occasion, yes."

Hoping curiosity didn't kill her, Eloise ejected the question burning the back of her throat. "Have you dated any clients?"

"I date every one of them for the hour they are there."

Yeah, she regretted tossing out the question, and she wasn't enough of a masochist to ask how many *'every one of them'* was.

"Why the long face?"

"Nothing." She plastered on a smile. "I was just thinking." Savannah had invited her out for a drink, and she'd delivered. She had no reason to feel like she'd just had the rug ripped out from under her.

"Thinking this was a date?" Savannah said.

"How did you—"

"It's my job to read your body language."

"Yeah, well, you're not at work now, so you can quit doing that."

Her smile was infuriating. Eloise wanted to lean across the table and wipe it clean off her face…with her lips. And mouth. And tongue. Definitely tongue.

Time for a change of topic. "You know your beers?"

"I wouldn't say that, but when I do drink, it's my preferred drop."

That was good to know. If she ever had Savannah over for dinner, she could buy some beer.

"Let me guess. You normally drink wine."

"Correct. By the bottleful." If she opened one, it wasn't often she didn't finish it.

"I like wine, but I drank enough of it as a teenager to put me off for life." Savannah's expression was wistful, or was that regret lurking in her eyes? It was hard to tell in the dim lighting of the bar.

"Your mum didn't mind you drinking?" Eloise asked.

She'd been allowed the odd glass of wine on special occasions, but she never got drunk as a teen. The good girl in her wouldn't let her disappoint her parents like that.

"Oh, Mum minded all right." Savannah shook her head, a look of defeat marring her features. "I was shown the door."

"How old were you?" Eloise asked gently, unable to imagine turning her back on either of her kids. If Mackenzie disobeyed her and secretly got trashed with her mates, there would be consequences, but kicking her to the kerb wouldn't be one of them.

"Eighteen." She looked up, regret shining in her eyes. "I wasn't a good person, Eloise."

"Teenagers are reckless."

"They can be. But it was more than that."

A charged silence settled between them. Savannah picked up a beer from the paddle, took a mouthful and put it back down. Eloise did the same. This one had a hint of lemon and…was that thyme? She could ask, but she didn't want to talk about beer. She wanted to know more about Savannah. What put the sadness in her eyes?

Then it hit her. "You were eighteen when your sister died." That would be enough to make most teenagers go off the rails.

Hell, it would be enough to make most people drink. Even so, that was a hell of a time to kick someone out. Her opinion of the grey-haired woman who came to the games—Savannah's mother—was lowering by the second.

"Leilani was a baby," Savannah continued. "Mum took her in, and instead of helping, I acted like a selfish arsehole."

"You were hurting."

Savannah laughed without humour. "I wasn't feeling anything. I was so high on pot and booze, I was practically comatose. Mum warned me if I didn't get it together, she would kick me out. She had Leilani to take care of and didn't need my crap on top of grieving the loss of her eldest daughter. But I was too far up my own arse to stop to think other people were hurting."

Despite the heavy mood, Eloise couldn't help but tease her. "You know that's not physically possible?"

"Are you sure?" Savannah waggled two fingers.

"Not an image I needed." To each their own, but sticking her fingers up her butt wasn't her idea of fun. "Where did you get the pot and booze from?"

"My sister's mates. I partied with them to celebrate Brooke's life, but we forgot to stop. They took me in when Mum locked me out. I slept on the floor at their flat, hanging out with a group of wasters. And I mean that in the literal sense. They were wasted all the time. None of them worked. Their dole money was spent on booze. We drank more than we ate, and it took its toll. My clothes hung off me, and I stank. But I didn't care. I just wanted the pain to go away."

Where was the man of the house? Eloise's father would've dragged her arse home if she'd ever tried to pull anything like that, grieving or not. "What about your dad?"

She huffed out a laugh. "What about him? He fled when I was a toddler. Never heard from him again until Brooke died. He wanted to have a relationship with me before it was too late. I told him to fuck off, it was already too late. My opinion on that hasn't changed over the years."

"I'm sorry you went through all of that." In comparison, Eloise had lived a charmed life. "But you're all right now, right? You and your mum?"

The sparkle in her eyes returned. "More than. She threw the tough-love card at me, and I love her for it. I probably would've resented her if she'd dragged me home, and she had enough on her plate as it was."

"That doesn't make you a bad person. Given the circumstances."

"That is what makes me a bad person. I should've been more supportive, instead of adding to Mum's stress."

"Teenagers are self-absorbed." Eloise continued to be the voice of reason. Just because she'd never stepped out of line didn't mean she couldn't see how losing a sibling as a teen could make someone strong-willed act out.

"Getting arrested for shoplifting was the best thing that ever happened to me."

Stunned, Eloise's poker-face dropped to the table like a deck of cards. Face up. "You have a record?"

"Not anymore. The slate gets wiped clean after seven years—if you have no more offences. Which I haven't. As I said, I wasn't a good person."

"Desperation doesn't make you a bad person." Eloise squeezed her hand. "What did you nick?"

"Tampons."

That was not what she'd expected, but somehow it made it less…what was the word she was looking for? Sinister? Calculated? "The essentials, huh?"

"Yep. But if I hadn't been drinking away my pitiful pay cheque, I would've been able to do the lawful thing instead of an awful thing to get *the essentials*." She put air quotes around the last two words.

"So, what happened after the arrest? Did you get tossed in the paddy wagon and shipped off to the station?"

"I did. And haven't you heard enough about me?"

"Not at all." Quite the opposite. She was enthralled.

And even a little bit excited to be living through Savannah vicariously. She wished she'd had the guts to do something daring. Perhaps not illegal, but nevertheless, a morbid part of her had always wondered what it would be like to be arrested.

Handcuffed and frisked. Okay, her mind was heading down a dangerously sexy path.

She gave her attention back to Savannah.

"I'll never forget the look of disappointment in Mum's eyes when she picked me up from the cop shop. Anger would've been better, but the whispered 'let's get you home' cut deep. She put me in the shower, fed me, and oh my God, being back in my bed, sleeping between crisp, clean sheets that smelled of lavender was almost a bigger high than the booze."

Her glee was infectious. It was also a reminder not to take the simple things in life for granted.

"For a week, I did nothing but eat and sleep. Once I could get out of bed without shaking like a haunted shithouse, Mum stood me in front of the mirror and told me to take a good hard look at myself."

"A sight for sore eyes," Eloise said.

"Indeed." Savannah put her empty glass on the table. "But a scary sight. I had bags under my eyes, my hair was limp, and my clothes hung off me. But worse than that, I had a haunted, vacant look.

"But that didn't scare me because I felt dead. Then Leilani stumbled into the bedroom." Savannah's gaze was distant as if she was recalling the memory. "Mum looked at me and said, 'Think of the example you're setting for her. Do you think your sister would want that?' Leilani handed me her dolly, and I was a goner. The poor kid was an orphan, and I had a mother with love to spare, yet I was acting like my life had ended the day my sister died. Fuck me." Savannah blew out a breath, raising the hair on her forehead. "That's some heavy shit. Sorry for dumping that on you."

"You have nothing to be sorry for. I'm honoured you could share that with me. I hope it helped somehow."

"I wouldn't say it helped—"

"Ouch." Eloise winced.

"I didn't mean it like that. It was a long time ago, and I've made my peace with it." Savannah sat back, arms over her chest, her intense gaze boring a hole into Eloise. "There's something special about you."

Unsure how to respond, she let out a nervous chuckle. She was plain. Boring. Compliant. "How so?"

"I haven't told that story to a soul in more than a decade. It's not something I'm proud of."

"But our past shapes us, and from where I'm sitting, it looks like you're in pretty good shape."

"Eloise. Are you flirting with me?"

Relaxing, she managed what she hoped was a flirty smile. "I think I might be."

Savannah's gaze turned from attentive to smouldering. "Come home with me."

Should she play hard to get? Act coy? Think about her answer? No way. She was too old to play games, and this was the best possible outcome Eloise could've hoped for.

She grabbed her jacket and stood. The pub was full to capacity, people talking loudly to be heard over each other, but she'd been so focused on Savannah, it felt like they were alone, shut in a soundproof room.

"Lead the way."

Chapter 14

The drive from the pub to Savannah's took less than ten minutes. It was a stone's throw away from Libellule's and not at all what Eloise had expected. Small was the first word that came to mind.

The kitchen and living area were one big space, with cream walls, tan carpet and ivory drapes. Why she'd expected gilded mirrors, expensive ornaments and plush furniture was beyond her. No, she knew why. Her expectations were based on fiction, and she needed to stop that.

Savannah was a unique, beautiful woman, not something made of fairy tales. Or was she? Because this all felt like a fairy tale. Things like this — standing in the home of the woman she desired staring at her with lust in her eyes — didn't happen to Eloise.

"Nice house."

"Thanks. Can I take your jacket?"

"Sure." Eloise slid it down her arms and handed it over.

Savannah placed it on a hook by the back door and hung her leather jacket beside it. They overlapped, and all Eloise could think of was taking a piece of Savannah's scent home with her.

"Let me show you around." She pointed. "Kitchen."

"I can see that." Turning, Eloise followed Savannah into the hallway.

She nodded at the two doors opposite them. "Bathroom."

Why did the mention of the bathroom make her want to pee? Badly. The beer she'd consumed didn't help. The urge grew stronger, making her clench her thighs.

"May I?" She nodded towards the bathroom door.

"Just a sec." Savannah reached inside, grabbed something off the back of the door and tucked it under her top.

"What's that?" Eloise wanted in on the joke.

"Gift from my niece."

"Show me."

"No!"

"Yes."

Smiling, Savannah handed it over.

It was shaped like a Do Not Disturb sign, but the words were more amusing.

Pooping. Please come back later.

"Charming." She handed it back. "I won't need it."

There was nothing sexy about the comment, but Savannah's eyes smouldered. She grabbed Eloise by the scruff of her jersey and pulled her forward. They were so close, when she spoke, her breath feathered over Eloise's lips. "Feel free to freshen up. Towels and flannels are on the shelf."

If that wasn't an indirect offer, Eloise didn't know what was.

Light-grey face cloths contrasted nicely with the dark-grey towels. After using the loo and having a quick wash, she dumped the used linen in the wicker clothes basket and opened the door.

"Fuck." She clutched her chest. "You're like a ghost."

"I assure you, again, I'm very much alive." Savannah captured Eloise's lips, turning her into a puddle right there in the hallway. She tasted like hops and lust. Her perfume was something sweet and musky. Something distinctly Savannah.

She pointed to the door on her right. "My room." She paused. "And you know where the living room is. Your choice." With that cryptic comment, she slipped into the bathroom and closed the door.

Fuck! Eloise raked a hand through her hair. Once again, she was completely out of her league. Savannah was a dominant woman, so why wasn't she issuing orders? Perhaps that was a role she played at work while in her own home, she was as vanilla as Eloise's favourite ice cream.

She could do vanilla. She'd done it all her adult life. But what if she'd read the comment wrong and Savannah went back out to the living room?

When the bathroom door clicked open, she jumped. She'd been so lost in her head, she was yet to move.

"You're still here?"

"Yep." She chuckled nervously. "Never done a runner before." Running out on Dominique didn't count.

"Not what I meant." She ran a thumb over Eloise's bottom lip. "I would like nothing more than to make love to you."

Eloise's breath hitched and her pussy throbbed.

"There's just one thing."

Of course there was. Eloise deflated. "Go on."

"I don't have any dental dams."

What did that mean? Eloise could only think of one reason, and it didn't bode well with her. "You don't practice safe sex at home?"

"It's called safer sex because—"

"Nothing is foolproof," Eloise finished for her.

"Wanna tell me about it?"

"No." The last thing she wanted to talk about right then was the night she lost her virginity and the broken condom that resulted in an unwanted marriage. Unwanted marriage, not unwanted pregnancy because there'd never been any question whether she would keep the baby.

Holding both her body and eyes captive, Savannah continued, "I don't have any dental dams because I don't bring women home. I don't do relationships, Eloise. I don't know how." Before she could reply, Savannah gave her a self-deprecating smile. "There I go being a downer again."

The only thing she'd done was let down her walls, and now that Eloise had a foot in, she wasn't backing out. "The only thing you're killing right now is my libido."

Savannah tipped her head back and laughed. "Lucky for you, or unlucky, depending on how you look at it, I don't have any implements here either. I have restraints, though."

Because that's what you like, isn't it, Eloise? She could've sworn Savannah uttered those words, but her lips had stopped moving.

"Do you know what I'd really like?" Savannah asked.

"Me?" Wonderful. Could she say anything cornier? Apparently, that third beer she'd sampled had broken her filter.

"Very much so." Savannah pushed Eloise's jersey up her torso, her gaze questioning.

With no doubt in her mind, Eloise raised her arms and leaned forward, letting Savannah remove her top. Cool air hit her skin, and she shivered with anticipation.

"Cold?"

"No." The temperature at Savannah's was cooler than she was used to, but it didn't matter. Her body was on fire.

With their eyes locked, Savannah backed her into the bedroom. Eloise's legs hit the foot of the bed, and she toppled backwards, bouncing on the mattress.

She was still giggling when Savannah tugged on the hem of her jeans and pulled them off along with her underwear. Unable to tear her gaze off Savannah, she watched her strip. It wasn't a frantic undressing, clothes flying as she'd expected.

It was slow and controlled, every movement deliberate. She lowered one bra strap at a time, removing the lacy material at a teasingly slow pace. After pulling on the zipper of her jeans, up, down, up, down, three times, she peeled them down her legs, flinging them aside.

She slid onto the bed and Eloise burst out laughing. "You've got socks on."

"Oh, yeah." She grinned, rubbing her sock-covered feet up and down Eloise's calves. "I have a client—" Her eyes went wide. "Never mind. Bad timing."

"It's fine." Eloise loved the normalcy of their conversation. Their tummies bumping together and legs entwined didn't hurt either.

Besides, this was something she had to get used to. Couples talked about their jobs. Maybe not just before sex. Although, it wouldn't be the first time she'd thought about work while having sex. But that was pre-divorce.

"Tell me."

"Not now. We have more pressing matters to deal with." Savannah punctuated the comment with a thrust of her thigh between Eloise's legs.

She groaned, resisting the urge to hump it like a bitch in heat. The simple act of skin on skin, the feel of soft curves against her own, was enough to drive her insane with desire.

The serious look in Savannah's eyes took the edge off Eloise's arousal.

"This might be an uncomfortable conversation, but it's necessary."

"Okay."

She stroked Eloise's cheek. "You truly are beautiful."

"Yep, that was uncomfortable." She laughed.

"Goodness. You're on fire."

"In more than one sense of the word."

"Good to know. So I'll make this as quick and painless as possible. Practising safer sex is paramount in my line of work."

Eloise knew that, so she nodded, continuing to run the backs of her fingers up and down Savannah's side, relishing in the feel of her soft skin and the dip of her waist.

"My last test was two weeks ago, and I haven't had unprotected sex, so I'm confident I'm clean. Now for the uncomfortable part."

Eloise swallowed, hand instantly stilling.

"Has there been anyone else for you?"

"No!" Her answer was probably a little too strong, but she hated that Savannah had to ask. Did she think she slept around?

You met with Domme101 with that thought in mind. Reminding herself of that, she flopped onto her back and flung an arm over her eyes.

"Hey." Savannah lifted her arm. "I told you it would be uncomfortable. But we're adults, responsible adults, so I had to ask. You don't have to reply, but without an answer, we can't—"

"There's been no one. I've slept with two people in my life. One I married."

"Is that a thing with you? Marrying people you have sex with?"

And just like that, any feelings of awkwardness vanished.

Returning her smile, Savannah kissed her softly. "May I make love to you?"

The desire in her eyes ignited Eloise's libido like a match to a candle, flickering brightly, burning hot.

Chapter 15

Several orgasms later, Eloise stared up at the ceiling, feeling more content than she had in a long time. The bedside lamp cast an orange glow over the room. While she'd still been trying to catch her breath, Savannah had pulled the duvet up to their waists.

Eloise suspected it was more for her sake, and she appreciated Savannah's thoughtfulness. She was a complex woman. Firm yet gentle. Confident yet vulnerable.

"Tell me about this." She traced the outline of Savannah's tattoo—an intricate design of flowers, leaves, birds, and abstract designs.

"The flowers and leaves signify beauty and growth." Savannah rotated her arm, pointing to pieces of the tattoo as she spoke. "And the sparrows, for me at least, are an expression of a free spirit and open-mindedness."

"It's beautiful. I like that it has meaning."

"Like me, it's been a work in progress. Sparrows are also symbolic of teamwork and enjoying the simple things in life."

"Is that why your house is so modest?" Eloise asked.

"My house is modest because my mother's isn't."

Confused, Eloise drew her eyebrows together. "Is that like being fed too many pickles as a kid and developing an aversion?"

"No. That was broad beans for me."

"Ick." That was one vegetable Eloise had refused to eat as a kid and still couldn't stomach. She would rather drink dishwater.

"It's not quite the same. A good chunk of my pay goes towards taking care of Mum and Leilani. It has since she took me back in."

"Guilt." Mortified she'd let that slip, Eloise slapped a hand over her mouth. "Sorry. I didn't mean to say that."

"It's fine. And you might be right, but I've never thought of it that way. Growing up, we were poor. Most of our clothes were hand-me-downs or bought from second-hand stores. Brooke and I were teased at school." She shrugged like it was no big deal, but it must have been tough. "Neither of us had the chance to go to college because we couldn't afford it. Knowing that didn't bother me, though, because learning didn't come easily." Another lift of her shoulder. "I basically went to school to eat my lunch, which wasn't much. Vegemite sandwiches. Cheap bread…" She tossed back the duvet and flung her long legs over the side of the bed. "And that's enough about me. I have food, and we can't live on sex alone."

"Pity." Eloise climbed out behind her, picking up clothes and tossing them on as she went.

Fifteen minutes later, they were sitting on the sofa with a plate of nachos balanced on a tray between them.

"Tell me about you," Savannah said as she raised a loaded corn chip to her mouth, hand underneath to catch any drips.

"I'm thirty-six. Divorced."

"Man?"

"Correct." She scooped some salsa onto a corn chip.

"Bisexual?"

"No." Eloise shook her head. "I don't think so."

"You don't know?" Savannah pulled two chips apart, breaking the string of cheese joining them.

"Let's put it this way. If I never have to see another penis, I'll be a happy woman."

"What about a replica…attached to a harness instead of a man?"

She would like to say her heart tripped and her pussy throbbed, but it didn't. "Maybe I'm broken."

"Self-loathing isn't attractive, Eloise."

The reprimand, although said with compassion, made her wish she could take her words back. Since she couldn't, she tried again, giving a more direct answer. "No, strap-on sex doesn't appeal to me. Is that an issue?"

"Not at all." Savannah shovelled some more food into her mouth, chewed and swallowed. "I'm very adaptable. What I won't tolerate is someone playing along because they think that pleases me."

"Isn't that what you do, though? At work." That was direct, but they were having a candid conversation, so why not?

"Fair comment, but no. We have a choice about who we do and don't see. As I was going to say earlier, I have a client who is into feet."

Unable to see the appeal, Eloise grimaced.

"Have you ever had your toes sucked?"

"No." She curled her toes into the carpet. "I'm very protective of my feet." She hated having them touched. Just the thought of a pedicure made her squirm.

"Back to what I was saying." Savannah paused. "Although, if you have a thing about podophilia, perhaps we should stop while the—"

"Pod-oh what?"

"It's the term for someone with a foot fetish."

"I wasn't uncomfortable. It's just not for me."

"Right, and that brings me back to your original question. We all have a choice, and I turn down any requests that make me uncomfortable—be it a kink or a fetish."

"Is there a difference?" Even as she asked, she pondered the question. "I mean, I'd say I'm into kink." She crunched on another nacho.

The plate was almost empty, which was a good thing because if there was more Eloise would just keep eating.

"Why?" Savannah asked after a brief silence.

"Why what?"

"What makes you say you're into kink versus having a fetish?"

"For one, I don't want to suck your toes." Eloise picked up her glass and downed the rest of her drink.

"You're on the right track, but I'm not going to say anything is absolute." Savannah dusted the crumbs off her hands and sat back. "Kink is something that may or may not be included during sex to enhance pleasure—bondage, discipline, restraints, blindfolds, sensation play. You get the picture."

Eloise nodded, confirming she got the picture and was into kink.

"A fetish is something that is inextricably linked to one's sexual behaviour. Typically, it's a focus on an object or a body part. Latex, leather…feet." She put the empty tray on the coffee table and flung her legs across Eloise's lap.

"How do you sleep on the couch?" Being close to six foot, she would have to curl into a ball to fit.

"I don't. Why? Is that something you do?"

"I used to," Eloise said. "When I first left Anton." It'd taken her a while to get used to sleeping alone again.

Savannah snickered. "I shouldn't laugh because I don't have anything to go by. But isn't that something people normally do when their marriage is on the rocks?"

"Probably. But I never did that." They'd put on a show that everything was peachy right to the very end. Had she known what else had been going on in their marital bed, that would've been a completely different story.

"What happened?" Savannah's voice was soft.

"We broke up."

"Okay." A hint of hurt flashed in her eyes. "If you don't want to tell me, you don't have to." She went to fling her legs off, but Eloise stopped her, trapping them under her forearms like a vice.

"He cheated."

"That had to hurt."

The comment surprised Eloise. Most people were too busy calling him every name under the sun to consider her feelings. Most people also didn't know what she was about to confess. Not only that, she didn't deserve their sympathy.

"I knew." Guilt clawed its way up the back of her throat, leaving a bitter taste.

"Yet you stayed?" Savannah freed her legs and sat up, sitting sideways on the sofa. "I'm not judging."

She knew that, and that was what gave her the courage to continue. "Our marriage had been loveless for years, but I chose to stay for the kids. It wasn't a hardship. He was a good provider, and we had a good life."

"He sounds like a prince." Savannah poked her in the side, making her smile.

"He was, for a time." The comment she'd made before they got onto kink and fetishes came back to her. "Which brings me back to saying I was broken. And you're right—self-loathing isn't becoming."

"Sorry."

"Don't be. It wasn't that I believed his words. My lack of interest in sex was because of his gender."

"'Cause he had a pee-pee?"

"Stop it." Eloise laughed, loving Savannah's ability to make her smile when her heart was heavy. "The first time I suspected he'd cheated, I felt relieved."

"Because you didn't have to sleep with him," Savannah said, and she couldn't have been more on the mark.

"You're good at this."

She smiled, her hands continuing to draw circles over the back of Eloise's hand. "Go on."

"It was like an unspoken agreement. He could have an affair as long as he was discreet and didn't bring it home." Her stomach twisted—a knot of anguish curling tighter and tighter. "Then he did."

"And you caught them?" Savannah asked gently.

"No." She shook her head; disgust, pain and regret slamming into her. "His daughter did."

"Oh, Eloise. Fuck." Savannah scrubbed her face. "How old was she?"

"Thirteen." She'd come this far, she might as well lay it all on the line. "Caught him fucking the neighbour's daughter, balls deep, in—or should I say on—our bed."

"Jesus. That's some fucked-up shit."

"You're telling me. I don't think Mackenzie will ever forgive him, and I'll never forgive myself for the part I played in it."

"Oh, kinky." She waggled her eyebrows, making Eloise laugh again.

"He suggested it once." She'd considered it for all of five minutes. Mainly because she would get to be with a woman, but she knew when that day came, because it was inevitable it would, it wasn't something she wanted to share with Anton.

Savannah linked their hands again. "How old was your neighbour's daughter?"

"Eighteen. Legal." That was something. "Mackenzie used to look up to her."

"Do her parents know?"

"No. I didn't see the point in ruining their lives too, and I'm sure Anton never told them, considering he wasn't man enough to tell me himself."

Savannah's eyes went wide, hand flying to her mouth. "Please don't say what I think you're going to say."

"Okay, I won't." She smiled to mask the pain squeezing her heart.

Compassion shined in Savannah's eyes. She held Eloise's gaze, waiting for her to continue.

"My normally outgoing daughter became distant and sullen. It took close to a month, but I finally wore her down. Anton had been emotionally blackmailing her. Told her it would be all her fault if the family broke up. She wasn't overly worried about that, but when he played the Jack card, it was enough to buy her silence."

"Your son?"

"Correct. And he doesn't know until this day. Although Mackenzie was only thirteen, she was insistent he never know." She smiled wryly. "And Jack still thinks his father's golden." Exhausted, she heaved out a long breath. "I didn't mean to dump that on you."

"It seems like we have more in common than two sisters."

"You mean verbal diarrhoea?" She'd been going for funny, but Savannah's expression was serious.

"I mean we are both strong women, who have been through tough times and come out better for it."

"I don't know if what happened to me made me a better person."

"How can you say that?" Savannah's gaze was intense. "A lot of women in your shoes would've screamed his betrayal from the rooftops, trying to paint him as the villain, without a care for who got hurt in the process. From what you've told me, you've done your best to protect your children, even if that means Jack thinks his old man is the shits."

"He was good to the kids, and that's all that mattered."

"Was?" Savannah asked.

"He's still good to Jack. Too good, I think. But Mackenzie barely speaks to him."

"Can you blame her?"

"No. But adults make mistakes, and she only has one father." She paused.

"If anything was to happen to him before they reconcile, I'd hate her to have to live with regret. But how do you tell that to a teenager?"

"I have an opinion on that, but I don't know you well enough to voice it, so I'm going to hold my tongue."

Eloise's first instinct was to harrumph, but Savannah was being honest with her, so she deserved the same respect in return. "I'm interested in what you have to say, but I'm also ready to put this conversation to bed." She gave her a small smile. "No offence."

"None taken." Savannah stood. "Speaking of bed. I have to be up by seven."

What was the time? Eloise looked at her watch, surprised to see it was after eleven. Where had the time gone? Four hours? Poof, gone in the blink of an eye. And a tangle of sheets. And an explosive orgasm. Nachos. Talking.

Okay, they'd squeezed a lot into those hours.

Reluctantly, Eloise stood. "Thank you for tonight. I had fun."

"Me too." Savannah helped Eloise into her jacket. "I would ask you to—"

"Don't—" Eloise pressed a finger to her lips. A bold move, but one she felt she could make when they were on equal footing.

Savannah lifted Eloise's hand and drew her finger into her mouth, circling her tongue around the digit.

"Don't," she uttered for a second time.

"Feels good, doesn't it?" Her eyes sparkled.

"Very." It was like a direct line to her clit.

Savannah's smile grew. "Like having your toes sucked."

"Ugh." Eloise slapped her hands over her ears. "Let's not ruin a good night."

"Speaking of…" She pulled Eloise to her and kissed her softly. "Goodnight."

"Night."

"Text me when you get home." She rocked on her sock-covered heels. "You know, so I know you got there safely."

Touched by the hint of vulnerability in Savannah's gaze, Eloise nodded. "I will."

Chapter 16

As promised, Eloise texted Savannah to let her know she got home in one piece. Not as easy as it sounded when she was flying high, drunk on lust.

Over the following week, they fell into a routine of sorts, messaging each other daily. Most of the time it was just everyday stuff—the weather, work, soccer—and Eloise soaked up every word.

The front door to her ex-marital home opened and Jack ambled down the driveway, lugging his backpack as if it weighed a tonne. It was Friday afternoon, and although Anton was out of town for the weekend, she had no desire to set foot on the property.

When Jack reached the car, Eloise pushed open the passenger door. "Hey, son."

"Hi." He dumped his bag on the back seat and climbed in the front.

After checking for traffic, Eloise headed back down the hill towards the lake. "How was school?"

"Good." He thumbed his phone, staring at it as if she was a taxi driver he didn't want to talk to. She got it, but it still annoyed the crap out of her.

Her irritation was quickly replaced by a smell so repugnant it burned the back of her throat. *What the hell is that?* "Did you shower today?"

"Huh?" Jack frowned, a deep crease appearing between his eyebrows. God, he looked like his father when he did that. "You're acting weird again."

"Sorry, but something smells." Once the road was clear, Eloise turned right onto Lake Terrace. "What's in your bag?"

"Clothes."

She stopped herself from asking if they'd been washed. Once they were home, she would do his laundry. Instead of interrogating him further, she opened the window, gulping in some fresh air.

"Is something bothering you?"

"No." He didn't look up.

Putting it down to hormones, she let it go. Besides, it was hard to talk when you were trying not to breathe. The smell was growing stronger by the second, scorching her nasal passages.

"Here we are." As soon as she shut off the engine, Eloise was out of the car.

She yanked open the back door and grabbed Jack's pack, beating him to it. Against her better judgement, she sniffed.

Fighting the urge to gag, she batted the air. "What the hell is that?"

Distracted by his phone, Jack answered, "I think Ratbag p—" Seeming to realise what he'd said, his eyes went wide, all the colour draining from his face.

What. The. Fuck!

Tamping down the fury that surged, Eloise fought to keep her voice calm. "Pardon me?"

"I meant Sooty. Logan's cat. I think she peed on it."

Not buying it for a second, she set her jaw. "Don't you dare lie to me."

"Mum." He looked stricken. "Dad will kill me."

"Not if I do first." She shook her head. There was no need to scare the kid. "Sorry. No one's going to kill anyone. Let's go inside where it's warmer."

She started towards the house. Jack followed, head hung low as if he was about to meet his maker.

"Put it in there." She pointed to the laundry.

His clothes and bag would be getting washed before they went anywhere near his room, but they could wait.

"Tell me what happened to your bag. The truth this time."

"Mum," he pleaded. "Dad's going to go apeshit."

"Let me worry about your father."

He swallowed, throat working, distress putting some colour back in his cheeks. "I'm so sorry. Kenzie's going to kill me too."

They'd always been close, so she really hoped that didn't happen. "Start at the beginning."

"You know how Ratbag went missing?"

"Yes." How could she forget? Her heart had been broken right alongside her daughter's.

"She's at our place." His eyes were full of worry. "Dad said not to tell you. That it would serve you both right for leaving us."

Anger simmered beneath the surface, but she pushed it down. "I did not leave *you*, Jack. You chose to stay with your father." Something she'd been adamantly against while hoping one day he would make his own choice to return to his mother's side.

"I know. But that's what Dad said, and he's going to be pissed. Please don't tell him you know."

Jack had texted earlier in the week to say Anton couldn't take him to rugby this Saturday and to ask if she could. She'd always divided her time between her kids' sports and often caught the end of one or the other's game, but tomorrow she would miss Mackenzie's soccer match and, by extension, seeing Savannah.

Having this dumped on top of that was a craptacular way to kick off her weekend.

Making a split-second decision, Eloise grabbed her keys. "Get in the car."

"What? No. Please don't take me home." He remained rooted to the spot. "I said I'm sorry."

"When will your father be back?"

"Sunday morning."

"Good. Get in the car."

"What are you going to do?"

"We're going to get her."

He groaned as she hustled him out the door, whining all the way. "Mum, please! Stop. You're going to ruin my whole life."

If the situation wasn't so serious, she would've told him to stop being so melodramatic, but there was nothing funny about what her bastard of an ex had done—asked Jack to lie to his sister.

And the sad thing was, she was about to do the same because Mackenzie could never know. Her father had hurt her enough.

Perhaps it was the planets aligning. Now brother and sister would each have a secret they kept from the other. Not out of deceit like Anton, but out of love.

She had taught her children not to lie, but sometimes, it was okay to keep a secret, especially if that was kinder than telling the truth.

As she drove back along Lake Terrace, following the route they'd taken five minutes earlier, she formulated a plan. She would not let Anton cause a rift between the kids.

Half an hour later, they were back home. The washing was on the line, Jack's bag flapping in the wind, and Ratbag was back where she belonged— lying in front of the fire, fast asleep after sniffing out her surroundings.

A car door banged, and Eloise glanced out the kitchen window. Mackenzie flung her school bag over her shoulder and waved bye to Bobby's mum.

"Kenzie's here." She used Jack's name for her. "Act excited."

"I know, I know." He appeared in the kitchen.

The door opened, and Mackenzie grinned at her brother. "Hey, Jacko Wacko."

"Hey, Kenzie kooties." He stole a glance over his shoulder. Eloise did the same, hoping Ratbag didn't wander into the kitchen before Jack had a chance to spill the beans.

"Guess what?" he said.

"What?" She looked from brother to mother, suspicion growing.

"Something really exciting happened today. You'll never guess. It's like a miracle."

Don't oversell it, Jack.

Eloise nudged him. "Just tell her."

"Ratbag came home."

"What?" Her mouth fell open. "If this is a joke?" She looked at Eloise, hope tinged with disbelief shining in her eyes.

"Come see." Jack pulled her into the living room.

Eloise followed, her heart in her throat, her oesophagus thick with emotion.

"Oh my God. My baby." Mackenzie practically fell on her. "Where have you been?" She pulled Ratbag onto her lap. "Wow, I can't believe you're here." She held her up, tears streaming down her cheeks as she stared the big fluff ball in the face. "I'm never letting you outside again."

Once, Eloise would've said that wouldn't be fair on the cat, but if she'd been locked up at Anton's, she was sure Ratbag would be fine.

Jack gave Eloise a coy smile, and she squeezed his shoulder. He hadn't told her the truth, but in the end, he hadn't had to lie to his sister either.

He sat beside Mackenzie, legs crossed. They exchanged a smile, and Eloise's heart melted. She would never stoop low enough to bad-mouth her ex in front of her kids, but she hoped it wouldn't be long before Jack saw his father for what he was—a deceitful man who cared about no one but himself.

***

Parked in front of the house she'd once called home, Eloise stared numbly. It felt like a lifetime ago since it'd been a home full of love and laughter. Once, she could look at the house and see nothing but her kids' smiling faces.

Now, the mere sight of it sickened her. It was like looking at a house where there'd been a family tragedy and wondering how anyone could live there.

She'd been naïve to think one day she would walk away and they would part ways on amicable terms. But she also never could've imagined just how ugly it would get.

Yesterday, while the kids were getting cleaned up after Saturday morning sports, she'd slipped outside and phoned Anton.

He'd sounded as happy to hear from her as she was to be talking to him. After a heated conversation where Eloise had danced around the real reason she needed to see him, he'd finally agreed to meet her at his place.

Preparing for battle, she marched along the garden path. He must've been watching her out the window because she'd no sooner lifted a hand to knock when the door opened.

It was tempting to knock anyway. *Tap, tap,* right on the bridge of his nose. With the satisfying image of him standing there with a bloody nose, she stared him down. "The cat."

"What cat?"

"Don't play me for a fool."

His lips kicked up, and she wanted to slap the smug look off his face.

Deep breaths, Eloise. She inhaled deeply and exhaled slowly. "You might think you're clever, but you're not. I heard you've turned into a miserable bastard, but asking your son to lie! That's a new kind of low."

He puffed his chest out. "Chip off the old block."

Perplexed, she shook her head in disgust. "You're actually proud of yourself?"

"Ratbag liked it here. It's not like I kidnapped her."

"But you held her captive." Her voice was shrill.

He scoffed. "Is that all? You got what you wanted."

"No, Anton. You're the one who always gets—"

A car sped down the street, drowning out her words. Anton watched it go, then eyed her from the top step. "You were saying?"

There was that smarmy look she'd lived with for the last ten years of their marriage. She'd lost count of how many times she'd walked away from it rather than subject the kids to a heated argument, but they weren't there this time.

"You drove one child away."

"Just a min—"

She silenced him with a finger. "Don't do it to another. Jack is terrified to come home. So, this is how I see it playing out. You're going to act all surprised and butt hurt that Ratbag must've got out.

"Then in a couple of weeks, when he's done what his sister did for months, gone looking for her to keep up the ruse, he'll get a text from me to say she turned up at our place."

"Why the elaborate plan?"

"Because Mackenzie doesn't know the part you played in this...or the part her brother played."

"So many lies." He clucked his tongue.

She didn't know whether to feel anger, disgust or pity for this man. To be honest, she felt all three. In her heart, she'd hoped that one day Mackenzie and her father would rebuild their relationship, but right now, she wasn't so sure that was a good idea.

"If you don't want to lose your son as well, I suggest you play along."

Hoping that hit home, she strolled back down the garden path, head held high despite the death glare she could feel like a hot poker between her shoulder blades.

When she dropped Jack off that night, she parked in the driveway and accompanied him to the door. If he thought it was odd, he didn't say. Anton shot her a snotty look, but when he turned to close the door and she heard him say, "Sorry, mate. Ratbag got out," she strode back to the car with a smile on her face.

It was a small victory; one she would take.

Chapter 17

Work had kicked her arse, and all Eloise wanted to do was put her feet up. Inside, she unbuttoned her jacket and wandered into the living room. The fire was almost out, but at least Mackenzie had made an effort to light it.

Poker in hand, Eloise stirred the embers and tossed on a piece of old-man pine. Denser than ordinary pine, it burned for longer and put out more heat.

Once the log caught, Eloise sank into her recliner and closed her eyes. She'd had a prick of a time balancing payroll, and they felt gritty after staring at the computer for so long.

"Can Bobby come over for tea?" Mackenzie's voice roused Eloise.

She popped her eyes open, watching her daughter descend the stairs. "It's a school night."

"So? She doesn't have to stay late. Her mum said she'll pick her up at eight."

"Is that right?" Eloise linked her hands across her stomach. "So this has already been decided?"

"Please." Mackenzie dragged out the word. "She's dying to meet Ratbag."

"Send her a photo."

"Fine." Mackenzie flung herself onto the couch.

The sulking act didn't work on Eloise, but there was a conversation they needed to have, and it would help if her daughter wasn't sullen. Besides, could a bit of compromise hurt?

"On two conditions."

She bolted upright. "I'm listening."

"You and I need to talk first."

Groaning, she slumped back again, hands disappearing into her oversized jersey. "What have I done now?"

"I don't know. You tell me."

"Nothing," Mackenzie said.

"Good. That was easy, wasn't it?"

"You're weird."

She'd heard the term so many times now, she'd come to expect it. "Secondly, you and Bobby cook tea."

"I only know how to cook two things."

"Spaghetti is fine." She didn't feel like anything heavy, and Mackenzie's version of spaghetti was cooking a pot full of noodles and adding a jar of pasta sauce. "Tell her six o'clock."

"That's an hour—"

Eloise gave Mackenzie a look that must've conveyed her words. *Take it or leave it.*

Her thumbs flew over her phone, and she dropped it beside her.

"Where's Ratbag?" Eloise moved from the sofa and perched on the coffee table, putting herself on eye level with Mackenzie.

"What's that look for? Am I in trouble?"

"Not at all. I asked about Ratbag."

"Yeah, but you have that look."

Eloise smiled at her daughter. She was growing up fast and was far too intuitive. She always knew when Eloise was getting ready to give her a speech, but that wasn't what this was about.

"You know how you were seeing a boy and now you're dating a girl?"

"Awkward."

It wasn't her finest moment, but she was struggling with a way to kick off the conversation. It was like the knot in her stomach had worked its way up her throat and twisted around her tongue.

The thought alone made her roll her tongue.

"You're acting weird again."

"Sorry, but I'm really nervous."

"What? Why?" Mackenzie leaned forward, elbows on her knees, nose inches from Eloise. "You're scaring me. Did something happen to Jack? Was Dad a dick?"

More than she would ever know. Ratbag appeared at that moment and jumped up beside Mackenzie. She curled up and started purring loudly when Mackenzie stroked her.

"I'm glad she's home," Mackenzie said.

"Me too." A happy silence fell as they both gazed at Ratbag. Aborting her mission, Eloise stood.

"Mum?"

"Yes?" She looked down at Mackenzie.

"What were you going to say?"

Sucking up some courage, she sat again. "You know how when we talked about Bobby…" Eloise held up a hand before Mackenzie could say 'awkward' again.

"And you said it's the twenty-first century and people don't come out these days."

Confusion knitted Mackenzie's brow, but she didn't interrupt.

"That's not always the case. Especially for older people."

"Yeah, well…" She shrugged. "I guess old people, like Grandma, would find it weird. But you said you were cool with it. And you're not *that* old."

Eloise returned her grin. If she was going to do this, it had to be now. While the atmosphere was relaxed. "This might be hard to hear." She swallowed the lump in her throat. "But your mum's…she's. Your mum's…"

Mackenzie watched her with both intrigue and uncertainty, then her mouth fell open, tears forming in her eyes. "You're not dying, are you?"

Way to go, El. She'd bungled this for so long, her daughter now thought she was terminal. "No, honey. I'm gay."

There. Fuck. She'd said it.

Stunned, Mackenzie slumped back on the sofa, hand clutching her forehead. "Did I hear you right?"

"Yes. I like women." It was easier to say that time. And why wouldn't it be? She no longer had anything to hide. Not from her daughter, anyway.

"Since when?"

"Always."

"But you married a man."

"I know."

"Why?"

"I got pregnant, with you." She took Mackenzie's hand in hers, every memory, every maternal instinct that would make her lie down and die for her children, shooting to the surface. "I was nineteen. Most guys would have run, but your father proposed to me."

"How noble." The sarcasm wasn't as thick as normal, but it was still there.

"Oh, Mackenzie. He was. He wanted you just as much as I did. Less than a year later, Jack came along, and we were a family. I would've done anything for you kids."

"Including marrying a man."

Eloise nodded. "Including that."

"He's still a cheat."

"He is, but adults make mistakes."

"It's pretty hard to unsee."

"I know, and I'm so very sorry for that." It was her biggest regret. "If I could change it, I would."

"Not your fault."

To a degree, it was. But Mackenzie didn't need to hear about her parents' pitiful sex life or Eloise's reluctance to confront him. That was adult shit, not something to dump on your child.

They'd also gone way off track. "So, you heard what I said?"

"Yeah. You're gay. Doesn't matter to me."

"You won't be embarrassed if your mother starts dating women?" There was only one woman she wanted to date, but she wasn't ready to confess to that yet.

Her eyebrows drew together. "Why would I be?"

Not wanting to lie, Eloise leaned forward. Mackenzie did the same, wrapping her arms around Eloise's neck.

"You know Dad's going to flip?" She sounded amused by the idea. Not surprising, really. She would probably find great joy in watching her father feel reduced by the fact his ex-wife liked women. Because make no mistake, Mackenzie was right. Eloise could not see him taking the news well, but that was none of her concern. She'd spent most of her adult life keeping him happy, and that door was now firmly closed.

"I do. And he'll probably think I've turned you."

Mackenzie unfolded her legs. "I'm not a zombie." She stood. "And I don't care what he thinks. Nor should you."

At times, Eloise wondered who was the adult here. It was equally amusing and scary. Mackenzie was too young to be adulting.

***

There was a knock at the door, and Mackenzie couldn't get there fast enough. She tore through the kitchen and skidded to a stop before yanking it open to a smiling Bobby.

They exchanged a quick kiss, and Mackenzie turned, looking like a giddy teenager in love.

"Hi, Mrs Carter."

"Hi, Bobby. Nice to see you."

"Can I tell her?" Mackenzie asked.

Eloise nodded.

"Mum just came out," she said in a rush.

"Out of where?"

"The closet."

Bobby's eyes went wide. "You put your mother in a closet?"

"No!" Mackenzie sounded exasperated.

Bobby bumped her shoulder. "I get it." She turned to Eloise. "Congrats."

Not what she'd expected, but entertaining nonetheless. "Thanks."

"You could date Coach," Bobby said. "I think she's swings that way."

"Nice idea." Eloise played along.

"No freaking way. No way." Mackenzie paced the kitchen, dragging a hand through her hair. "No way. Not happening."

"Why? What would be so bad about that?" Hoping Mackenzie was just being dramatic, Eloise kept her tone light. But if she was dead serious, she didn't know what she would do. In a roundabout way, having her daughter had already dictated who she dated — married — once. She couldn't allow that to happen again.

"She's my coach, and half the team have the hots for her. They will hate me."

"Will not." Bobby linked their hands. "Ignore her, Mrs C. They're all too young for Ms Sloane." She turned to Mackenzie, amusement sparkling in her eyes. "Have you ever noticed that sounds like schlong?"

"All right, you two! Kitchen."

Chapter 18

Who knew having your nails done by a professional could be so therapeutic? When Savannah had texted Eloise and offered to treat her to a manicure, she'd been both thrilled and apprehensive.

Her poker-face was flimsy at best, and she'd felt like everyone would know about her and Savannah. But once she got there, Savannah had acted like the professional she was, and it'd been easy to relax and enjoy being pampered.

It was the first time Eloise had had a manicure and probably wouldn't be the last. For some reason, she'd always thought it was a waste of money, yet she'd paid ten times that amount for sex.

"Oh, fancy." Martha glanced at Eloise's hand as she retrieved a lever-arch file to dump last week's timesheets in. Wages were done online, payslips sent out electronically, but the factory staff still used paper timesheets.

"Thanks." She looked at her nails, admiring the pink and red swirls.

"What's the occasion?"

"No occasion. Just treating myself." The white lie hadn't been intentional, but what else was she supposed to say? A woman she was falling for had treated her to a manicure, complete with flirty looks and the brush of their legs under the table?

Martha glanced around as if to make sure no one else was listening. "Who is he?"

"No man."

"Woman?"

Fuck. Was the world really that PC now and Eloise hadn't noticed? Nah, she didn't think it was that. This was just Martha being Martha — the least judgemental person she'd ever worked with.

It was also the perfect opportunity to come out at work. But was it fair to come out to a workmate before telling her family? Was there an order you were supposed to do this?

Like a dog scenting gossip, Taylor appeared beside them. "What are you two gasbagging about?"

"You." Martha grinned.

"My nails." Eloise wiggled her fingers.

"Ooh, nice. Where did you get them done?"

Unsure if that was information she should be sharing, Eloise hesitated. Libellule's fronted as a beauty parlour, so there was probably no reason she shouldn't, but it felt like her own little piece of paradise. Something she wanted to keep for herself.

The phone rang, and Martha answered it. Taylor wandered off, confirming she hadn't really given a crap about where Eloise had her nails done, and the moment to come out at work was lost.

That was both disappointing and a relief. If she'd told Martha first, she would've felt disloyal to her parents. But before she worried about that, it was time to come clean with Mackenzie about who she was seeing.

Over the past week, she'd asked more questions about Eloise being attracted to women, and with any luck, she'd had enough time to digest that news before Eloise dropped the next bomb.

***

Later that night, as they cleaned up from dinner, Eloise broached the subject. "I'm going out Saturday night."

"Can I come?" Mackenzie asked.

Damn. Perhaps her casual way of starting the conversation hadn't been such a bright idea after all. "Why would you want to do that?"

"Because Janelle makes the best pie."

"Who said I'm going to Janelle's?" Eloise tossed the dishcloth in the sink.

"That's the only place you go. Wait!" Mackenzie spun around, her full attention on Eloise. "Are you going on a date?"

There was no going back now. "I am."

"Cool. Who with? Is she nice?"

Absolutely stunning. Sexy, charismatic and humble. She kept hold of those words and threw out Mackenzie's descriptors instead. "You might think she's a bit of a hard-arse."

"Ugh." Mackenzie fed a piece of leftover chicken to Ratbag. "Do you know what Ms Sloane made us do at practice?"

"What?"

"We had to do a stupid fitness drill."

"Why is that stupid?" Eloise asked. "I would think being fit is a good idea."

"Going for a run keeps me fit."

"And when was the last time you did that?"

"I do it all the time. At practice." Seeming to forget what they'd been talking about, Mackenzie turned to leave the kitchen.

"Where are you going?"

"I've got homework."

"It can wait." A knot of anxiety coiled in Eloise's stomach. "We need to talk."

Groaning, Mackenzie flopped into a chair at the kitchen table and sprawled across it as if she was already in pain.

"Don't be a drama-llama."

"Then don't start a conversation like that. I already know it's going to be painful."

Hoping that wasn't the case, Eloise pulled out a chair at the table. "You know how you came out?"

"Yes, Mother." Mackenzie's voice was droll.

"And then I did."

"Yes, Mother."

"Stop." Eloise laughed.

"Well, get to the point. You're gay. You're going on a date. I'm not the one having an issue with that."

God, this kid was fifteen going on thirty-five.

"Are you saying I have an issue with it?"

"Do you?"

"No."

"Then get to the point." Her hand snaked out, brushing Eloise's fingers — a barely-there touch of comfort.

Mackenzie could act as indifferent as she liked, but she was as protective of her mother as Eloise was of her.

"You know how your coach is a bit of a hard-arse?"

"Yes." That had her attention. She was all ears, her gaze locked on Eloise.

Ratbag meowed at their feet, and without breaking eye contact, Mackenzie hauled her into her lap.

"How would you feel if I went on a date with her?"

"I thought you said you *are* going on a date." She was back to being sullen. "So what does it matter what I think?"

"Because I fucked up once and I don't want to do it again."

"Mum!"

She never dropped the F-bomb around her kids, so Mackenzie's outburst wasn't surprising.

"Well, it's true. What you think matters a great deal to me." That wasn't to say she would cancel their date, but she would be disappointed.

Eloise put up a hand, blocking Ratbag when she tried to climb onto the table.

"When did this happen?" Mackenzie asked.

"What?"

"This date thing. Were you hitting on my coach at soccer?"

"No!" She shook her head adamantly.

That was the furthest thing from the truth, but she couldn't tell Mackenzie the whole truth either. That would mean outing Savannah as a sex worker—something she would never do. "Did you know she's a beauty therapist?"

"No, but that makes sense. Leilani has the coolest nails." She dropped her gaze to Eloise's hands. "Did she do yours?"

"Yes."

"And you asked her out on a date?"

"Yes." Not a lie.

"Wow, go you."

"So you're okay with it?"

A worry line appeared. "Are you going to be all smoochy with her at soccer?"

It was tempting to tease Mackenzie, but now wasn't the time. "Soccer will be the same as usual. I promise I won't embarrass you, and I'm sure Savannah will keep being the coach you know."

"The coach half the team has the hots for." Mackenzie peered at Eloise through a lock of hair that had fallen across her face. "And you've just crushed their hearts."

"As I said, it will be soccer as usual."

"Does Leilani know?"

That was a very good question. "I'm not sure. But I can ask if you like."

"Nah. I'll find out soon enough."

"So you're okay with it?"

Another shrug. "I just want you to be happy."

"And that's all I've ever wanted for you." They stood, and Eloise hugged Mackenzie fiercely, sandwiching Ratbag between them. She meowed, and they broke apart, smiling.

"Now that you know, I'm going to start coming out to other people."

It was time to kick the closet door off its hinges and embrace whatever came her way. The good and the bad, because she was bound to encounter both.

"Can I tell Jack?" Mackenzie asked.

"No."

She coughed into her hand. "Closet."

"Mackenzie, would you stop?" She would tell Jack when she was good and ready.

"Can I have alcohol at my party?"

"No." She wasn't budging on that.

"Can Bobby sleep in my room?"

Infuriating bloody kid. "Don't you have homework to do?"

Chapter 19

Excited anticipation put a pep in Eloise's step as she strode along Savannah's driveway. Other than being invited over, she had no idea what the night ahead would bring. She didn't care, as long as she got to spend it with Savannah.

There was still so much to learn about each other. For some reason, they'd freely dumped the worst moments of their lives on one another. Tonight, though, she hoped to keep the conversation light.

She also hoped they were going somewhere quiet, so they didn't have to yell to be heard over the noise. Savannah had been tight-lipped about that. *Dress casually* was the only clue she'd given, which wasn't much of a clue at all.

Staring at the wooden door, Eloise knocked and waited, bouncing on her toes to keep warm. Mount Ruapehu had received a good dusting of snow during the week, and even though the mountain was a hundred kilometres away, she could feel it at ground level.

The door popped open, and Savannah greeted her with a beaming smile. She wore leggings, thick socks, and a long-sleeve shirt, and her hair was braided in two ponytails. She looked like she was having a sleepover, not about to go on a date.

"Am I early?" Eloise glanced at her watch. She wasn't, but something was off. "Are you sick?"

"Nope and nope." Savannah dragged Eloise inside, closed the door and nailed her to it, pinning her against the wood with her body. "I've wanted to do this since you kept throwing me flirty glances, looking the picture of innocence while I painted your nails."

"I did —"

She was going to say *not*, but the word was swallowed by an open-mouthed kiss. Savannah tasted like apples and strawberries, and she smelt like…popcorn? What the hell?

"What's going on?"

"I thought we'd have a pyjama party. Reinvent our teenage years."

That sounded like a fantastic idea, but there was a small problem. "I didn't bring my PJs."

Without a word, Savannah picked up a gift-wrapped box and handed it over.

"What's this?" If it was an extravagant gift, she didn't know if she could accept it.

"I believe the words you are looking for are *thank you*."

"Thank you." Eloise perched on the edge of the sofa and untied the big black bow on top. "You didn't have to buy me anything."

"I kind of did." She sat beside Eloise and bumped shoulders. "Open it."

Red satin swam in her vision as soon as she lifted the lid. "It's just what I wanted," she said with exaggerated enthusiasm. She placed the cami top on her lap and pulled out the satin pants with a drawstring waist. "I love them. Thank you."

"You're welcome." Savannah glanced up at the heat pump. "Is it warm enough for you in here?"

"More than."

"Good. Go try them on. I'll pour the drinks and load a movie."

It'd been a long time since she'd had a pyjama party, and that had been with her sisters. "You're serious?"

"Serious as a cockroach."

"They're just creepy."

"I'm allergic to them," Savannah said over her shoulder as she headed for the kitchen.

Was that even a thing? "Are you messing with me?" Eloise asked.

"Not at all." Savannah grabbed two glasses out of the cupboard. "When I was living in squalor, I constantly had a stuffy nose and ear infections. I thought it was from sleeping on the floor and eating poorly. Turns out, I'm allergic to cockroaches."

"I'm not even going to ask how you discovered that."

"Good. We have a pyjama party to kick off." She pointed to the hallway. "Now, go."

"Yes, ma'am." Eloise spun on her heels, squealing in surprise when Savannah grabbed a handful of her backside.

In the bathroom, she wondered what she was doing there. She could've just stripped in the living room. But since she was there, she took the opportunity to learn more about Savannah. Sure, she'd used the bathroom before, but she hadn't lingered.

The room was compact with little clutter. Off-white walls, gold fixtures, oval mirror above the vanity. No toothbrush or make-up lying around.

She glanced at the corner shelf above the toilet. There were candles on either side of a potted plant. She stood on tippytoes, getting a closer look at the foliage flowing over the sides. Hearts. The leaves were shaped like hearts.

A bang on the door startled her. "You okay in there?"

That would teach her for dawdling. "Yep. Won't be a second."

When Eloise emerged, she was greeted by a shrill whistle. Savannah raked an appreciative gaze over her, and Eloise returned the favour.

While she'd been taking her sweet time in the bathroom, Savannah had changed into a similar outfit to the one she'd given Eloise, except the satin pyjama pants and cami top were black. The braids were gone, and her hair now tumbled around her shoulders in thick, black waves.

Savannah licked her lips. "Who was I fooling thinking I would be able to keep my hands to myself if you weren't parading around in a sexy little negligée?"

They each took a step, meeting in the middle of the room. It was a gentle kiss. A slow exploration as if they had all the time in the world. Savannah kissed her mouth, her lips, her neck before nibbling on her earlobe. Eloise melted into her, her body responding like it always did, desperate for more.

"Right. Movie." Savannah pulled away, her face lighting up with glee when a groan escaped Eloise.

As she floated back down to earth, a framed picture caught her eye. Two teens were standing on a wooden walkway, steam and mud pools bubbling around them. They were far from fashion statements—their ratty clothes giving testament to a poor upbringing—but they looked like the happiest two girls in the world.

"You and Brooke?" Eloise asked.

"Yeah." Savannah's gaze was warm as if she was living a happy memory. "I was thirteen. Brooke had just turned sixteen. As a little kid, all she wanted to do was go to Orakei Korako's Geothermal Park, but we couldn't afford it."

"Is it expensive?" Eloise asked, dragging her gaze from the picture to Savannah.

"Define expensive. Fifty dollars is spare change for some families and the difference between whether you eat or not for others."

"Sorry." Eloise gave Savannah an apologetic smile. "I didn't mean to be insensitive."

"Nor did I. My comment wasn't said to make you feel bad. For the average family, no, I guess it's not expensive. But at the time, any outings were to places that didn't cost anything." Her smile returned. "And we went to a lot of places. We had a good life. Mum's a good mother. Anyway, Brooke spent her first pay cheque on a family day out." She looked at the picture. "And that was it."

"Great memory to have."

"I have many." Savannah handed her a glass. "And hopefully by the end of the night, you'll have a few to take home with you."

She didn't doubt that for a second. Every minute she spent with Savannah went directly to her memory bank. The one she kept sealed like a vault, and she was the only one with a key, free to crack it open and stare at them like treasured jewels.

***

With a movie playing, they sat amongst a pile of blankets and pillows and sipped on rose cider. It had a coral pink hue, and the berry notes made her tastebuds ping.

Eloise held up her glass. "This is good."

"I'm glad you like it. I had no idea where to start with wine."

"Didn't you say you used to drink wine?"

"I did," Savannah said. "By the boxful."

"Ew, nasty." Eloise screwed up her face, feeling like she was channelling Bobby.

"And just as bad coming back up," Savannah said.

"How did you afford it? The booze?" Eloise hoped she wasn't being too intrusive, but wine cost money, even the stuff in a plastic bladder shoved in a cask.

"I worked part-time at KFC until I got fired. Then I went on the dole."

Eloise didn't know a lot about the benefit, but being so young, Savannah would've had to prove her mother couldn't support her financially.

"How old were you when you had your first job?" Savannah asked Eloise.

"Twenty-six." She'd been in her last year at college when she got pregnant and didn't get her first full-time job until Jack started school.

"Wow. That's, like, ancient."

Eloise laughed. "You sound like Mackenzie."

"She's a good kid."

"So's Jack. They're my world."

"Mum and Leilani are mine. Everything I do is for them."

That sounded familiar. "We have that in common."

"It sounds like we have more things in common than we realise," Savannah said.

"Favourite food?" Eloise asked.

"Pasta."

"Same," Eloise said. "Favourite—"

"Uh-uh. My turn." Savannah tapped her lip thoughtfully. "Favourite holiday destination?"

"Queenstown."

"Have you been there?"

"Often." She flew there at least once a year. "My parents live there. You?"

Savannah grinned around her glass. "My mum lives here."

"Ha-ha, Smarty. Have you been to Queenstown?"

"Once. Mum always wanted to go there, so I surprised her for her birthday."

Eloise took a sip of her cider and put her glass on the coffee table behind them. "Did you pull out all the stops?"

"What's a holiday without going big?"

"Go big or go home." Eloise paused. "Tell me more."

"We went on the Milford Sound coach and nature cruise."

As she spoke, Eloise's eyes slid shut. Savannah's words transported her to the spectacular scenery, the wildlife, the sky-high mountains, the lush rainforests and the thundering waterfalls.

When she finished telling her tale, Eloise opened her eyes and met her gaze. "Sounds like you had a blast."

"We did. Leilani was only eight, and she still talks about it to this day." Savannah flicked back a blanket. "Are you peckish?"

"I am." Assuming they were going out, Eloise had left some money for Mackenzie and Jack to order pizza for tea, but she hadn't eaten herself.

Not that she could *eat* herself. Okay, that was enough cider. Eloise climbed out of the nest of blankets and followed Savannah to the kitchen.

The movie was still playing, but she had no idea what it was about, so it didn't matter. "Can I help with anything?"

"I've got it." Savannah pulled her head out of the fridge. "I probably should've asked before now, but do you have any allergies? Intolerances?"

"No allergies. A few intolerances, but not when it comes to food."

"Tell me about them."

"Cheats and liars."

"I'm with you on the liars, but not all cheats should be condemned. And before you get pissy"—her smile was too alluring to get riled up—"I'm not excusing your husband's actions."

"Ex-husband."

"Ooh, no comment about being pissy?"

"Nope. But I am intrigued what kind of cheating you think is okay." She kept her tone light, but her stomach was in knots. No matter how Savannah wanted to colour it, it wasn't something Eloise could get on board with.

"Do you know what a cuckold or cuckquean is?"

Of course she didn't. "No, but I'm sure you're about to tell me."

"Only if you want to know."

"Sure."

As if she'd been prepared for Eloise's reply, she didn't hesitate. "In a nutshell, a cuckold is the husband of an adulterous wife, and a cuckquean is the wife of an adulterous husband."

"So you're saying I'm a cuckquean?" She didn't think she was any kind of queen.

"You're more like a princess." She grinned. "But in the kink world, the cuck is aroused by his or her partner having sex with others." Savannah slid a platter onto the bench.

Cuck-whatever forgotten, Eloise's mouth salivated as she eyed up the selection of green grapes, red grapes, cheeses, salami and hummus. "This looks divine."

Savannah handed her a cheese knife. "Be my guest."

Chapter 20

By the time the movie ended, Eloise still had no idea what it had been about, but she was pleasantly relaxed and didn't want to move. Sometime after they'd eaten, she'd gravitated towards Savannah, toppling sideways until her head was in Savannah's lap.

"Did you like that?" Savannah muted the television.

"It was great."

"What was it about?" There was a smile in her voice.

"You got me." Reluctantly, Eloise hauled herself up. "It's your fault. Having my hair stroked always puts me to sleep."

"Interesting, yet stroking you elsewhere wakes you up."

"You got me again," Eloise said, hyperaware of how delicious the satin pyjama pants felt against her skin.

"I got you something else." Savannah extricated herself from their blanket fort.

Eloise peered over the top of the pillow, watching her retrieve yet another rectangular box. This one was black with a red ribbon around it.

"Red symbolises passion, and black —"

"Symbolises death," Eloise interrupted, certain Savannah would be the death of her. Death by orgasm. Was that a thing?

"Black is a colour of mystique," Savannah continued. "It evokes elegance, sophistication and sexual prowess."

Feeling bold, Eloise twirled a lock of Savannah's hair around her finger. "Did you just describe yourself?"

Ignoring her, Savannah nodded at the box. "Open it."

Stalling, Eloise stared at the unopened present. She'd forgotten what it was like to have gifts lavished upon her, and although it felt good, it was hard to accept. "You really didn't have to buy me anything."

"If you won't open it, I will."

"No!" Feeling like a five-year-old about to have her favourite toy ripped out of her hands, Eloise held tight. Then it hit her. Was it a toy?

Was the temperature about to go up and their pants go down? If the anticipation rolling off Savannah was anything to go by, Eloise was on track.

She popped the lid off the box. Unsure what she was looking at, she lifted out a leather strip adorned with—she did a quick count—nine metal O-rings. "What is it?

"It's a reins body harness restraint." She took it from Eloise. "It can be worn at the front or the back of the body, depending on what you're comfortable with. And the D-rings mean we can experiment with high and low arm placements." A wicked grin lit up her face. "Or I can hog-tie you."

Fuck that. "Pickles."

"I thought that might be getting ahead of ourselves." Her smile grew. "But it was worth it to see the look on your face. It went from intrigue to desire to *what the fuck?*"

"I hope it now says *you are the most amazing woman I've ever met,*" Eloise said sincerely.

Savannah had the ability to draw any number of emotions out of her at any given time. Joy, desire, introspection, lust, and something deeper. Something she wasn't ready to dissect right then.

Putting aside the body harness, Savannah braced her hand on the floor and moved in for a kiss. Eloise met her halfway.

"It's nice having you here," Savannah said when they came up for air. "I feel really…horny."

Eloise laughed. She should add surprised to the list of things Savannah made her feel.

"Let's play a game?"

"Sure." Eloise nodded. "What's it called?"

"Savannah says."

"Sounds exciting. What are the rules?"

"You do what Savannah says or use your word. Which, may I remind you, is Marmite."

How had she forgotten that? *Terrible sub.* That's how. And the reminder just reiterated what she'd sensed from day one. She could trust Savannah to respect her mind and body. It was too soon to know how her heart would fair, so she opened the proverbial box she wasn't ready to unpack and slipped that inside.

"Savannah says, tell me what you're feeling?"

"Like a terrible sub. I mean, what kind of submissive can't remember her safe word?"

"An excitable one." She hooked a finger under the strap of Eloise's cami top and lowered it down her arm. "This needs to go."

Without question, Eloise pulled it over her head and tossed it aside. Time stood still as Savannah raked her gaze over Eloise's body, the fire in her eyes burning into her.

"Savannah says, no touching." She licked her lips and inched forward, taking a nipple into her mouth.

Resisting the urge to run her hands through Savannah's hair, Eloise tipped her head back, basking in the pleasure lavished upon her. Soft lips. No stubble. No race for the finish line. Just a lazy exploration.

Eloise shuddered with pleasure when Savannah moved her mouth to her other breast, tasting and nipping in turn, taking her sweet time teasing Eloise as she grew more and more frantic with desire.

With a smack of her lips, she released Eloise's nipple. When their gazes locked, her eyes were heavy with lust. "Savannah says, on your feet."

Obeying, Eloise got to her feet, wincing at the cold, damp feel of the satin pyjama pants between her thighs. Taking her underwear off when she'd changed had felt like the right thing to do, but she was starting to wonder. Whenever Savannah was near, it was like someone turned a tap on down there.

"Savannah says, strip." After issuing the command, Savannah crossed the room and dimmed the lights. The room fell into semi-darkness and with the turn of the dial, the atmosphere went from playful to sexually charged.

Once Eloise was naked, Savannah picked up the reins restraint body harness and held it between them by the padded collar. The tear of Velcro was loud in the otherwise quiet room. "Front or back?"

She appreciated being asked, but she also had no idea. Thoughts of losing her balance and faceplanting made the decision for her. "Front."

"Safe word?"

"Pick…" She cleared her throat. "Marmite."

Savannah secured the strips of Velcro around her neck. "Let's go back to Pickles. I would feel better if we did."

"Okay." She could do that.

Using it for a colour had been idiotic. She could see that now. The one good thing that had come out of that, though, was that she knew she only had to utter the word and all play would stop. No making her feel bad because she couldn't take more.

Savannah put two fingers underneath the leather collar, her knuckles brushing Eloise's skin. "Not too tight?"

She was tempted to make a strangled gurgle, but Savannah's foot on her toes banished the thought.

"Something funny?"

"No, Mistress."

"Good." Turning the collar, Savannah ran the leather strap down Eloise's back.

A complaint worked its way up her throat, but she swallowed it down, unsaid message received loud and clear. If she wanted to act like a brat, she would be treated like one.

"Hands behind your back."

Eloise obeyed, and the padded wrist cuffs looped around her left wrist, then her right.

"I could attach them here." She pulled Eloise's arms up between her shoulder blades. "Or here." She lowered them slightly. "But I think I'll attach them here." The click of the cuffs being attached to a D-ring echoed in her ears.

Once Savannah stepped back in front of her, Eloise tested out her range of movement. Her hands remained where they were—resting on the fleshy mound of her hips, just above her backside.

"Fucking beautiful." Savannah cupped Eloise's crotch at the same time as she sealed her lips over Eloise's mouth.

She wanted nothing more than to wrap her arms around Savannah, to pull her body flush against her own, but she could do nothing more than stand there completely at her mercy.

Eventually, Savannah broke the kiss. "On your knees."

A shiver of lust made Eloise's nipples harden in anticipation.

"Yes, Mistress." She sank to the floor, kneeling on the pile of blankets. Would Savannah push her onto her back, or would she strip and order Eloise to taste her?

She tossed a pillow in front of Eloise and tapped it with her toe. "Face here."

What the fuck? How was she supposed to do that with her hands behind her back?

"I've got you." Savannah grabbed the back of the harness and guided Eloise forward until she was face down and arse up, head tipped to the side.

She'd never felt so exposed, and she loved it. The anticipation was killing her. A week ago, the mere thought of an open-handed slap repelled her. Now, she welcomed it.

Face scrunched up, she braced herself for a blow that didn't come. Black pyjama pants landed on the carpet, followed by Savannah's cami top.

Saliva pooled in Eloise's mouth and moisture gathered between her thighs. Not knowing what was coming next was exhilarating.

With a sexy gleam in her eyes, Savannah moved to the rear until Eloise had to stop tracking her or go cross-eyed. Practically able to feel the sharp sting of an open-handed blow, Eloise braced herself. Would she buck and yelp or moan in pleasure?

Savannah's hands caressed her backside, but she didn't strike. Instead, she cupped her buttocks and buried her face between Eloise's thighs.

It was like nothing she'd ever experienced before. It was insanely hot, incredibly intimate and slightly embarrassing. She could only imagine how she looked with her arse in the air, face smashed against the pillow, hands bound behind her back.

The next lick of Savannah's tongue banished any thoughts of discomfort. Her sole focus was on the pleasure coursing through her body as Savannah ravished her, devouring her with her mouth, fucking her with her tongue.

When her orgasm struck, it was fierce, thundering through her with the force of a tidal wave, drowning her in ecstasy. She slid forward, until she was flat on her stomach, gasping and panting for breath. "Fuck. I think my ovaries exploded."

"*Thank you, Mistress* will suffice." Savannah freed her arms, taking her time to lower them to the floor before massaging Eloise's shoulders. "How do you feel?"

"Shattered." She rolled onto her back, basking in the cocoon of blankets and taking in Savannah's naked form—her taut abs, her belly button piercing, her gorgeous breasts and the sleeve of tattoos.

But beyond that, the sensual woman beneath the surface. The woman she needed to get her hands on.

She pushed up onto her knees. "How may I please you, Mistress?"

Without replying, Savannah hooked a finger under the collar and pulled Eloise to her, sealing their mouths together.

The kiss felt different to every other time. It wasn't sexual. It was something deeper.

Feelings! Feelings were involved. Eloise shuffled forward and held Savannah tight, breasts squishing together. "Are you okay?"

"Yep." She nodded. "Just processing."

"You're not confusing sex with love, are you?" Eloise joked, unsure whose heart she was trying to protect.

"No." Savannah unbuckled the harness and helped Eloise out of it, then wrapped a blanket around them both and rested her head on Eloise's shoulder. "I'm having feelings I don't know what to do with."

Eloise already knew Savannah was a beautiful woman. What she hadn't been prepared for was the vulnerable woman hidden beneath the incredible packaging.

She wanted to wrap her in her arms and tell her everything would be okay, but her mind was racing a mile a minute.

"I'm having those feelings too," she admitted, laying her heart on the line right beside Savannah's. She stared at the beige carpet, picturing two love hearts side-by-side.

The silence was comfortable, like when you were with your person, staring out at a beautiful landscape, and she didn't want to interrupt it.

Eventually, Savannah spoke. "I haven't dated since I was in my twenties, and I've been wary ever since."

"What happened?" Eloise asked gently.

"Blair, my one and only serious girlfriend, was fine with what I did when we first met. Then she got all possessive. I don't do possessive, Eloise. But I am loyal. When I love, I love hard. I would kill for my family." She gave Eloise a small smile. "Metaphorically, of course."

"Of course."

"Going back to your question. No, I'm not confusing love with sex. But I won't say the two are completely separate. For me, sex is an integral part of a loving relationship. It's also the first thing to go when a relationship breaks down. At least, that's what happened to me and Blair. Some nights when I got home from work, she could barely look at me." She tipped her head to the side. "There I go being a sad sack again."

"S.S. Sad-sack Savannah."

"Technically…" Savannah held up three fingers. "That's three Ss."

"Beauty and brains."

"They're Bs."

"Shut up." Eloise bumped her shoulder, the skin-on-skin contact reminding her she was naked beneath the blankets. She didn't want to move, but it was getting late, and she had teenagers to get home to. "I don't want to move, but I have to get going." She flicked back the blankets, feeling more at home in her own skin than she ever had.

The comfortable silence she'd enjoyed moments before turned heavy. The need to fill it tugged at her, but she resisted the urge, busying herself as they both got dressed.

She folded the red, satin pyjamas and held them out to Savannah. "Thanks for the PJ party. It was fun."

"Keep them. They're yours."

"Can I leave them here?" She blushed. "Fuck, that sounded presumptuous, didn't it?"

"Have I told you lately you're adorable?"

"Maybe." Eloise bit her lip, feeling like a giddy teenager. "And I would never try to change you." The funny thing was, when they were together, she didn't give Savannah's job any more thought than she gave her own.

In fact, it would be nice to be in a relationship with someone who didn't constantly bitch about their job. "You're perfect the way you are."

"Perfect might be a stretch." Savannah rocked on her heels. "One day, I hope to only do beauty therapy, but until Mum's house is freehold and I've paid for Leilani to go to college, I won't be—"

Eloise pressed a finger to her lips. "Slow down. I'm not asking you to change anything. A relationship should enhance your life, not smother who you are."

Wasn't hindsight great? Considering how long it'd taken Eloise to realise that, it was a big statement to be throwing around.

Savannah raised an eyebrow. "Speaking from experience?"

"I am, and although my ex has no idea that I repressed who I was to give our kids a better life, I would never ask someone to change who they are just to please me."

"You're not out to your ex?" Savannah asked.

"No." Eloise shook her head, the familiar knot tightening in her stomach. "I'm only out to my best friend, you and Mackenzie. I'm going to phone my parents this weekend." She would be seeing them at Christmas, but that was six months away.

"How did Mackenzie take the news."

"Fine." Eloise bit back a smile. "Until I told her I had a date with her coach."

"Seriously!" Savannah's mouth fell open. "So, she knows about..." She waved her hand between them. "This? You and me?"

"Is there a you and me?" Eloise asked, her heart pounding madly.

"That's the burning question, isn't it?" Savannah brushed Eloise's cheek. "I'd like to give it a try. If you're willing to take a chance on me."

Take a chance! Huh. She couldn't believe Savannah was willing to take a chance on *her*. It was equally exhilarating and terrifying. "I'd like to try. I'm also nervous as hell."

"You and me both." Savannah took Eloise's hands in hers. "Does that mean we're exclusive?"

Had she forgotten what she did for a job? "How does that work?"

"For me," Savannah said, "it's on an emotional level. I don't form attachments to my clients."

Amused, Eloise raised an eyebrow.

"Other than you." Savannah kissed her softly. "There's something special about you, and I don't want to mess this up."

"I'm sure if we keep the lines of communication open, we'll be fine."

"Agreed. And I don't do passive-aggressive. So if something's bothering you, tell me."

"I will. Promise." She'd had enough passive-aggressive behaviour to last her a lifetime.

Needing one more kiss, she pushed up on tippytoes. Savannah bent forward, and their lips met. Once, twice, three times.

Chapter 21

Blowing out a calming breath, Eloise grabbed her phone. Normally, she called her mother via video chat, but she didn't want to see her look of disappointment if this didn't go well.

Rain streaked the windows, the washing was drying on the clothes horse in front of the fire, and the kids were out.

"Hello?" Her mum answered on the third ring.

"Hi. It's me." Eloise sank into the recliner by the fire.

"I know who it is. How are you?"

She sounded happy and relaxed. A good start.

"I'm good."

"And the kids?"

"They're great. Has Mackenzie been in touch?"

"She has."

"And?" Eloise knew the answer, but it gave her something to talk about while she gathered her courage. School holidays were coming up—two weeks in July—and since she wasn't allowed alcohol at her party, Mackenzie had decided she wanted to spend her sixteenth birthday in Queenstown—home to ultimate adventure activities.

"That's fine. Of course it is," her mum said. "You know we love having her."

"Did she mention her friend?" Eloise asked.

"Girlfriend." She said it like it was no big deal.

What a relief. "And you're fine with her being in a relationship with a girl?"

"Pardon me? Did you say relationship, as in dating?" her mum asked.

Great, she'd put her foot in it, but her mother needed to know, especially if she had plans of putting them in the same room. "Yes, dating."

"Gotcha. And why do you sound so worried? It's the twenty-first century, you know?"

Yes, she knew. Mackenzie had told her.

"One of the guys I work with just got engaged to his boyfriend," her mum said. "Well, fiancé now. I told him I better get an invite to their wedding."

"How would you feel if it was your son?"

"I don't have a son."

Eloise laughed. Her mother was fifty-eight and sharp as a vampire glove. When Eloise had stumbled across one of those online, her immediate reaction was 'fuck that'. But then she'd looked closer…and wondered.

The soft, sexy leather gloves with sharp metal points on the fingers — said to create an intense, prickly sensation — were reportedly great for sensory play. And why the hell was she thinking about kink while talking to her mother?

She jumped off the sex train and back on the family train. "How would you feel if it was your daughter?" Eloise asked.

"Marrying a gay man?" her mum said. "You know that's unlikely."

Maybe she should've sucked it up and called her mother via messenger, so she could see her smiling face and her mother could see her exasperation. Or maybe not. Her heart was beating a rapid tempo at the mere thought of what she was about to say.

"What if your daughter was gay?"

"Which one?"

She was too on edge to continue with the jokes. "Me, Mum. I'm gay."

The silence that followed was deafening. Eloise pulled the phone from her ear and looked at it to make sure they were still connected. Normally, she had no problem waiting the other person out, but this was too painful.

"Say something, please." The despair she felt was clear in her voice.

She'd done everything she could not to disappoint her parents, and if her mother had an issue with her being attracted to women, she would be heartbroken. But she couldn't take the words back, and she didn't want to.

No matter what came her way, she would hold her head high. It was time to live the life she was meant to live. A life where she did things that made her happy instead of doing what made everyone else happy, often to her own detriment.

"Did you really think I'd love you any less?" The hurt in her mother's voice filled her with remorse and relief.

"No. You always told me you would love us no matter what."

If only she'd believed her parents would never turn their backs on her when she was nineteen, terrified she'd failed them, pregnant and unable to see any other option than marrying Anton.

"When did you realise you were gay?"

"Twenty years ago."

"What?!" She could practically see her mother shoot upright in her chair. "Oh, honey. You've kept this to yourself all this time?" Her voice was caring now. Motherly. "Is that why you broke up?"

"Yeah, kind of." She easily could've painted Anton as the bad guy here, a lesser person might have, but she wasn't blameless.

She also wasn't going to beat herself up about that again. "Will you tell Dad or should I?"

"He's right here."

"Hello?" Her father's gruff voice came down the line.

Her mother had a habit of playing pass-the-phone without telling you who was on the other end first.

"Hi, Dad. It's me."

"Hey, Spud. How are you?"

She smiled at the childhood nickname. Her two sisters, Amber and Jade, were known as Pumpkin and Sweet Pea. It would be fair to say her father was an avid gardener.

"I'm good. Mackenzie's looking forward to coming to stay."

"Bringing a friend, I hear."

"Yeah, Bobby. She's a good kid." Sixteen wasn't really a kid, but she wasn't a grown-up either. "And an excellent soccer player."

"I hear Squirt's back playing."

It would also be fair to say her dad had a thing for nicknames.

"She is, so make sure you've got a soccer ball handy for her and Bobby to kick around." It was the only practice they would get over the next two weeks.

"What kind of name is that for a girl?"

"It's actually Roberta, but don't call her that or I'll tell her to call you Jefferson." He went by Jeff, but knowing Bobby, she would call him Mr Wilson anyway.

"I was only joking. And I'm sure you didn't ring to discuss names. Wait, you're not pregnant, are you?"

"Not likely."

"You only have to sneeze and—"

"Dad!" He wasn't wrong, but that wasn't why she'd called. "I'm not pregnant. I'm seeing a woman." That came out easier than she'd expected, and it hadn't burned the back of her throat.

"What do you mean, seeing?"

Nothing like relaxing too soon. She didn't want to spell it out… Wait. She definitely should've video-called. Her dad was a pro at delivering questions with no tone, but his facial expressions always gave him away. "Are you teasing?"

"Oh, seeing-seeing. Like dating."

They weren't exactly dating, but it was more than sex. "It's early days yet."

"When do we get to meet her?"

"As I said, it's early days."

"Scared we'll scare her off?"

"You can't use scared twice in the same sentence. Mix it up a bit."

"Is that what you're doing?"

Although it was a fair comment, it stung. There was nothing wrong with being bisexual or questioning, but that wasn't what this was about. "No, Dad. I've always been attracted to women."

"But you married Anton."

"I married Anton," she confirmed.

"Why?"

"Remember that sneeze you mentioned?"

Her dad laughed, instantly lifting her mood. He hadn't laughed sixteen years ago when his nineteen-year-old daughter announced she was pregnant. But she was a grown woman now.

"Are you happy?" Gone was the jovial tone of her dad's voice. In its place was a love so strong she felt it radiating down the line.

"Extremely."

"Then I'm happy too."

"Thank you, Dad." Warmth enveloped her as if her father was standing right there in her living room.

"Does Anton know?"

"Not yet." She couldn't imagine anyone she'd told so far would've delivered the news.

"You know he's going to take a blow to his ego. But don't let him get to you. It's a man thing."

That was the least of her worries. Kind of. Sort of. It did play on her mind, but she was more concerned with how he would take the news when it eventually got back to him that Mackenzie was dating Bobby. If he said one negative thing, she would scratch his eyeballs out.

After a few more words with her dad, her mother was back on the line. "How's Ratbag?"

"Good." During the course of the phone call, she'd curled up in Eloise's lap. "It's like she was never gone."

"I still can't believe he did that to her."

That was one thing she'd happily vented about to anyone who would listen. For a time, her parents had thought Anton was the golden boy, but the brass coating was rubbing off, revealing the grey surface beneath.

"She's home now, and that's all that matters."

"You're a good person, honey. With a big heart. I hope you find yourself in this relationship instead of losing yourself."

Maybe her mother had been more aware of her misery all along. "Thank you for loving me for me."

"How could I not?" She sounded appalled. "You're my flesh and blood."

She appreciated the sentiment, but her heart twisted for Mackenzie all the same. Sometimes being flesh and blood wasn't enough to keep a relationship strong.

After ending the call, Eloise phoned her sisters. Amber, the baby of the family was fine. She even commented that she could see the appeal. An interesting remark, but Eloise didn't push for more.

Jade, the middle sister, wasn't as accepting. She said she was, but it was in her tone. And her bitchy comment. *We all have to live with the choices we make.*

That could be interpreted any number of ways, but Eloise hadn't bothered enquiring what she was getting at. There was no point. The main thing was, she was out to her family.

Chapter 22

After making sure Mackenzie and Bobby boarded the plane with no issues, Eloise wandered out of the terminal and headed for home. It was a bitterly cold July day, but that wasn't enough to dampen her spirits.

An entire week with no one to please but herself. Two months ago, that would've sounded like heaven. Now, though, life was more fulfilling when she was pleasing someone else.

As soon as she stepped inside, Ratbag jumped off the bench, weaving around Eloise's legs as if she hadn't just been licking the breakfast dishes.

That would teach her for not stacking the dishwasher before rushing out the door to make it to the airport by eight. She shrugged out of her jacket and picked up Ratbag. There was no point chastising her now; she wouldn't have any idea why she was in trouble. "I'm afraid you're stuck with me this week."

Her phone chirped and she put her down as fast as she'd picked her up. "Sorry, girl." She swiped the screen, her insides turning to mush when she saw who the text was from.

[Savannah] Hey, did Mackenzie get away okay?
[Eloise] Yep. What about Leilani?

Recently, she'd learned that Leilani's grandparents on her father's side had kept in contact over the years, but they'd also kept their distance for whatever reason. Perhaps seeing their deceased son's child was too painful for them, or maybe they simply hadn't wanted to disrupt Leilani's life any more than it already had been. But now that she was older, they were building a relationship, and she'd met an entire other family. Aunties, uncles and cousins.

[Savannah] Yep, three days in Ōtorohanga.

Eloise's mind flicked to the small town. When the kids were young, they'd spent a weekend there, checking out the Kiwi House and Native Bird Park before strolling down the main street and admiring the Kiwiana display gallery.

Her phone beeped with another message; this one from her bestie.

[Janelle] What are you doing tonight?

With any luck, seeing Savannah.

Before replying, she sent the same question to Savannah—*what are you doing tonight*? When no reply came, guilt gnawed at her insides. Janelle was a great friend and didn't deserve to be brushed off, so she sent a reply.

[Eloise] Not sure. Why's that?

[Janelle] Having cocktails and a potluck dinner for our anniversary. Come over. Bring that hot chicky babe of yours too.

Her phone dinged again, drawing Eloise's gaze to Savannah's name.

[Savannah] No plans, what about you?
[Eloise] Not sure.

Her phone rang, and she almost leapt out of her skin. "Fuck!" She punched the phone icon. "Yes?"

"Too soon?" Janelle asked.

"For?" The penny dropped. "Never mind." She'd have loved to introduce Savannah to her friends, but she wasn't sure if they were there yet. But how did you get there without taking that step? "I was about to ask her, but then someone called."

"Click," Janelle said.

"Don't you dare hang up on me." Eloise narrowed her eyes. Ratbag tilted her head as if that look was for her. "Who else will be there?" Eloise asked.

"Christopher and Alana."

She'd met Janelle's brother and wife a number of times over the years. Chris was a great guy, and his wife, whom he'd met while working around America, was a sweetheart. Although she'd been in New Zealand for close to ten years, she hadn't lost her accent.

"Frank and his girlfriend are coming too."

"Oh." The *oh* was as flat as a punctured tyre and laced with worry. She wasn't concerned about Carla, she'd seemed nice enough the one time Eloise met her, but as far as she knew, Frank and Anton were still good mates.

"He'll be fine," Janelle assured her. "I promise."

"Does he know I've been invited?"

"Yes."

"Does he know I'm—"

Janelle interrupted. "Seeing a woman? Yes."

If it'd been anyone else, she would've been pissed off. But Janelle was far from a gossip, so whatever she'd told them would've come from a good place.

"Carla's bisexual, so you don't have to worry about any judgement. They're looking forward to seeing you."

"Because I'm queer?" She sounded sullen and hated herself for it.

"Because I haven't told them how unattractive you look when you're sitting on the pity-pot, little girl panties around your ankles, waiting for someone to wipe your—"

"Stop." Laughing, she put her worries aside. Janelle had always had her back and always would. "By the way, happy anniversary."

"Thanks. It's not until next week. July tenth."

"You sound like your sister-in-law."

"Fine. Tenth of July."

"Better."

After ending the call, Eloise texted Savannah to see if it was okay to call. By the time she hung up, she had a date, and her day with no plans was suddenly busy.

***

Right on five, the knock came. Ratbag raced Eloise to the door as if she was a dog. "Nosy." She nudged her back with her foot and opened the door to the woman who'd changed her life and made her heart sing and girlie bits dance. Savannah looked as beautiful as ever, huddled into her black bomber jacket and wearing a beanie.

"Please, come in." Eloise stepped aside, feeling nervous now that she was there. What would she think of her home?

It was twice the size of Savannah's and nowhere near as tidy. It wasn't a pigsty, but it had the lived-in feel of a family home — PlayStation console in front of the TV, soccer ball in the corner, Ratbag's toys scattered around.

She glanced at the framed photos of Mackenzie and Jack adorning the walls. Her home spoke of the woman she was — a woman who adored being a mother.

"You must be Ratbag." Savannah crouched and held out a hand.

Almost in slow motion, Ratbag's back arched, her fur stood on end, and then she hissed before disappearing under the kitchen table.

"Ratbag!" Eloise stared at her in disbelief. "I'm so sorry. She's never done that." What the hell was her problem? Weren't pets supposed to be a good judge of character?

"It's fine." Savannah straightened to her full six foot. "She can probably smell Mum's cats on me."

"Cats?" Eloise asked, giving Ratbag the evil eye as she peered at them from under the table.

"Two Cymrics."

"Kim whats?"

"Cymrics. A longer-haired version of the Manx cat."

"No tail?"

"Correct." Savannah unzipped her jacket, revealing a grey knit top.

"Here, let me take that." Eloise took it and hung it on the coat tree by the back door. She would need it again soon.

"Shoes too?" Savannah gave her an amused grin.

"Clever." But they weren't at Libellule's, and it wasn't Eloise handing over her clothes. Tempting, but if they started down that road, they would never make it to Janelle's on time.

"Mind if I wash my hands?"

"Not at all." Eloise turned on the kitchen tap and nodded towards the soap dispenser she kept nearby. "Drink?"

"If you're having one."

Damn straight she was. It'd been a big week and it would take the edge off her nerves. "Wine or beer? I've got cider too, or juice. And, of course, there's water in the tap."

"A beer would be great, thanks."

"Coming up." Eloise opened the fridge and retrieved a bottle. By the time she turned back around, Savannah was sitting at the kitchen table and Ratbag was pawing her leg, trying to get up.

What the hell? Eloise shook her head in bewilderment. If she'd hissed because she could smell cats on Savannah, surely their scent was embedded in her clothes as well.

Maybe something happened to her at Anton's. "I'm sorry about before."

"It's fine. Like people, some cats take longer to warm to me."

She couldn't imagine anyone taking long to warm to Savannah, but the hint of vulnerability she let show now and then was shining through.

"Are you nervous? About going out?"

Savannah exhaled a heavy breath, chest rising and falling. "I don't normally get nervous around new people, but I'd be lying if I said I wasn't." She smiled shyly—a stark contrast to her put-together personality. "I don't want to let you down."

The declaration touched Eloise on so many levels. She'd spent her entire life worrying about letting other people down. Having those words said to her was a foreign concept.

"I don't think you could ever do that. And if it's any consolation, I'm nervous too." She was dreading seeing Frank. No doubt, the entire night would be relayed to Anton. But that also made her determined to let him see exactly how happy she was.

"Why would you be nervous?" Savannah asked.

"A mate of my ex's will be there."

"Does that mean I have to act a certain way? You know, keep my hands to myself so your ex doesn't know?"

"No fucking way!" That was the absolute last thing she wanted. "Wait." Eloise turned it into a joke. "Are you planning on groping me in front of everyone."

"Maybe." Savannah gave Eloise a flirty smile. Her grin was so damn sexy, it ploughed straight over top of Eloise's worries.

Ratbag went for Savannah's beer bottle, batting it with her paw. She tilted it towards the cat's mouth, letting some drip onto her tongue. She didn't look impressed, but she didn't jump off her lap either.

"Come on, girl. Down you get." Eloise shooed her off and grabbed the lint roller from under the kitchen sink. "Here." She held it out.

"Aren't you going to do the honours?" Savannah pushed the chair back and spread her thighs, her innocent smile speaking of nothing but mischief.

Taking the challenge, Eloise brushed the fur off Savannah's black jeans, making sure her pinkie finger grazed her clit in the process.

Savannah inhaled sharply. "You'll pay for that."

"Hey, I'm only doing what you asked."

Chapter 23

By the time Eloise pulled to a stop outside Janelle's, her nerves were performing an unwelcome tap dance in her belly.

"Ready?" she asked.

"Yep," Savannah said stoically. "They're just people, right? How hard can this be?"

After grabbing the container off the backseat, they hightailed it up the drive. Eloise had no sooner knocked when the door flew open.

Janelle welcomed her with a bone-crushing hug and a beaming smile. After releasing Eloise, she extended a hand to Savannah. "You must be the lady of the hour."

Although the slur hadn't been intentional, Eloise could've strangled her right then. Why she had a love for the term was anyone's guess.

Despite Savannah saying she was nervous about tonight, you wouldn't know it. She looked as calm and composed as ever. "And you must be the lady of the house. Nice to meet you."

Smiling, Janelle stepped aside. "Please, come in. It's colder than a polar bear's ice hole out there." She shut the door behind them.

"I see you're on fine form," Eloise said, amused despite having heard it before.

Grant appeared, looking as chipper as ever. "Hey, El." He gave her a side-on hug and turned to Savannah. "You must be Savannah."

"I am." She held out a hand, and they shook.

As soon as introductions were out of the way, Janelle looped her arm through Savannah's. "Come meet my brother and his wife, Alana. She's American, but we won't hold that against her."

Secure in the knowledge Savannah was in good hands, Eloise followed Grant into the kitchen. The oven was on, and the crockpot was plugged in next to the microwave. Stepping closer, Eloise breathed in the heady combination of orange and cinnamon. "Mulled wine?"

"Correct," Grant replied. "Would you like a glass?" He was a handsome man, clean-shaven with short, dark hair and the deepest blue eyes Eloise had ever seen.

"Please." She put the container of lolly cake on the bench and shrugged out of her jacket. "How much of that has your wife had?"

"Only one. You know how she gets when she's nervous."

"Overcompensates with jokes." It was a trait they both knew well.

Grant handed her a glass. "You're glowing. I'm happy for you."

"Me too." She took a sip of mulled wine, savouring the combination of flavours that made her tastebuds ping: orange, lemon, cinnamon, nutmeg, cloves and ginger.

"One for your lady?" At least he didn't call her the lady of the hour.

"Lovely offer, but Savannah's more of a beer drinker."

"A woman after my own heart."

A burst of laughter came from the living room, drawing Eloise's gaze that way. "I better go rescue my..." She paused, swallowed and tried again. "My girlfriend." It was the first time she'd said that aloud. It felt odd and fantastic at the same time. *My girlfriend.* She rolled the words around a few times, getting more comfortable with them.

Before she could move, Janelle appeared.

She reached for the bottle of beer Grant had just retrieved from the fridge. "The poor woman will die of thirst if she has to wait for you."

"Hey." Grant held tight. "I was getting there."

"Children, it's not a competition."

They looked at Eloise and burst out laughing. "Look at us, so eager to please."

That was something Eloise understood. Savannah had a quiet presence about her that made you want to please her, to make sure she was taken care of and happy. Speaking of, who the hell was looking after her?

Wine glass in hand, Eloise took the beer bottle from Grant and wandered into the living room.

Savannah looked right at home, sitting on the sofa, talking to Christopher and Alana, who sat opposite her on an identical two-seater. As if sensing Eloise's gaze on her, her lips pulled into a smile, but she didn't break eye contact, instead giving her full attention to Alana.

As unobtrusively as possible, Eloise sat beside her and handed her a drink. She mouthed "Thanks" and took a swig.

"It's different, for sure," Alana said, and Eloise wondered what they were talking about. "Especially not getting tips."

"I tipped you, babe."

"You did." Alana looked at Chris with love in her eyes.

"Is that how you met?" Savannah asked. "At the bar?"

"It is." Alana put her glass on the coffee table between them. "What about you? How long did you bartend for?"

"A couple of years."

That was news to Eloise, and she kicked herself for not asking more about Savannah's work history. Although, she hadn't discussed hers either. Work wasn't something they tended to talk about.

"What about you two?" Chris asked, his gaze flicking to Savannah's hand on Eloise's leg. "Where did you meet?"

Crap. Eloise kicked herself a second time. It was only a matter of time before someone asked the question, and they should've rehearsed a response before now.

"Good question," Grant said as he placed a cheesy spinach cob loaf on the coffee table. Eloise wanted to dig in, but she refrained.

"Frank and Carla are here," Janelle called out as she rushed to the door. It opened and banged closed, and the last two guests of the evening joined them.

"Everyone, this is Frank and Carla." Janelle made introductions. "You know my brother, Chris, and his wife, Alana."

"Hi," Chris and Alana said in unison. Chris stood, and the two men shook hands and clapped each other on the back. Why did blokes do that?

Probably the same reason Janelle hugs the stuffing out of you.

Oh, yeah.

She seriously needed to stop talking to herself before Frank thought she'd gone batty.

"And you remember Eloise?" Janelle said.

Plastering on a smile, Eloise turned in her seat. Although niceties were necessary, she hated them. She especially hated that everyone was looking at her. "Hi, Frank. It's good to see you."

It was the polite thing to say, but time would tell.

"This is Carla." He motioned to his girlfriend. Barely thirty at a guess, strawberry blonde, large breasts. Not that Eloise was looking, but her knit top was so tight, it was hard *not* to look. "You remember her?"

"Of course." Eloise returned Carla's smile, wondering if she remembered Eloise at all.

The first and only time they'd met had been at her ex-marital home about a month before she left Anton.

"And this is Savannah," Janelle said, all bright smiles and isn't-this-fun vibes radiating off her.

Frank extended a hand. "Nice to meet you."

"You too." Savannah stood, and Eloise tried not to laugh when she towered over him. Not by much. Maybe three or four inches, but size mattered to guys.

Carla extended a hand, and if Eloise wasn't mistaken, Savannah hesitated for a second before taking it. The shake was brief, but Eloise didn't miss the smirk Carla shot Savannah. What the hell was that about? Whatever it was, it set her teeth on edge.

***

By the time they sat down to eat, everyone was in good spirits, and Eloise wrote Carla's behaviour off as her imagination.

"How did you two meet?" Carla asked Christopher and Alana.

Great. They were back to this. Savannah nudged Eloise's leg under the table. Eloise nudged it back, acknowledging it was only a matter of time until the question landed on them. Again.

"I was doing my OE, working as a wrangler in the mighty USA"—Chris added a twang to the word wrangler—"I won gold for wrestling a bronc, and it was love at first hogtie."

Janelle smacked his arm. "You are so full of shit, little bro."

Alana leaned back in her chair, eyeing Chris with amusement. "Is that right, city boy? The way I recall it, you were piss drunk—"

"The saying is pissed—" Chris corrected her.

Ignoring him, Alana kept her gaze on Carla. "Chris used to come into the bar where I worked. I thought he was a tight-arse." She glanced at him. "Did I get that right?"

He nodded and held up a hand. "In fairness, I was still getting used to the whole tipping thing."

"True," Alana agreed. "And as the saying goes, the rest is history."

While everyone chatted, Janelle stacked empty plates. It didn't feel right sitting on her backside considering it was Janelle's anniversary, but Eloise knew from experience any offer of help would be met with resistance.

"What about you guys?" Alana asked, her gaze on Frank and Carla.

"She's my PA," Frank said.

What the hell? Eloise choked on her drink. Why hadn't Janelle told her that before now? Fucking your personal assistant was taking the title a little far. They could've shared a laugh at the very least.

"Cute. A workplace romance," Savannah said.

"Know something about those, do you?" Carla raised an eyebrow, but it wasn't a curious look. It was more of a challenge. Was she trying to one-up Savannah?

"I do. My sister met her boyfriend at work."

"How old's your sister?" Grant asked.

The question was innocent, but Eloise's heart sank all the same. Savannah had deftly dodged the question about them, but she'd walked into another land mine.

"Two years older than me." Savannah leaned her elbows on the table. "And a lady never tells her age."

Her powers of deflection were admirable. There was no reason she couldn't be honest, but if she had, the atmosphere would've gone from relaxed to heavy in the span of two words. *She's dead.*

"So, where did you two meet?" Carla sat back as Janelle took her empty plate.

"At the rubbish dump," Savannah said, her face devoid of emotion.

Taken aback, Eloise wasn't sure whether to laugh or shoot Savannah a look of outrage and come up with something more outrageous just for shits and giggles. And because something about Carla rubbed her the wrong way.

"Embarrassing." Eloise dropped her head into her hands and peered sideways at Savannah. "You said you wouldn't tell anyone."

"Come on, babe. You're not the only one who can't back a trailer."

"Oh, my God. They are the worst," Alana said. "So, what? She just got in your car and backed it up for you?"

"Yep, and as the saying goes…"

"The rest is history," Alana finished for Eloise.

With all the 'how did you meet?' questions out of the way, the conversation was more neutral.

Placing her empty glass on the table, Savannah leaned in close, her breath warm on the shell of Eloise's ear. "I need to use the bathroom?"

"Do you want me to come with you?" Eloise whispered back.

"Thanks. But I'll be fine."

Less than a minute after Savannah left the table, Carla stood. She whispered something to Frank, her gaze never leaving Eloise, and disappeared up the hallway.

A knot of unease curled in Eloise's stomach. She wanted to follow, but she had no good reason to. If she did, she would just look like a possessive, insecure girlfriend.

"She seems nice," Frank said.

"She is." Unsure if Frank was in on what Carla was up to, Eloise gave him a tight-lipped smile.

"Pudding anyone?" Janelle asked as she placed a selection of desserts on the table: lolly cake, apple pie, whipped cream and hokey-pokey ice cream.

A few seconds later, Savannah reappeared. She took her seat and shuffled it in.

"You okay?" Eloise asked.

She nodded, eyes on the table. "Ooh, is that lolly cake?"

"It is," Janelle said. "Did Eloise hide it from you?"

She hadn't hidden anything, and she hoped Savannah wasn't hiding anything from her either. And she really needed to take a pill and chill the fuck out.

By the time they finished dessert, including jelly shots, Janelle was three sheets to the wind and doing her best to get everyone up dancing.

She grabbed Eloise by the hand and pulled, but her butt remained glued to the sofa.

She hated dancing, even at small gatherings. The only time she got her groove on was when she'd had more than two drinks and no longer cared how uncoordinated she looked.

Janelle released her hand and pulled Savannah to her feet. They swayed to the beat like long-time dance partners. It was mesmerising. She'd been certain they would hit it off and she wasn't wrong.

The song changed and Eloise's heart hit the floor. Carla bumped Janelle out of the way and sidled up next to Savannah. She, too, put her arms above her head, swaying to the music and bumping against Savannah.

Before long, they were doing a seductive dance, circling each other and grinning. When the song ended, everyone clapped and cheered. Hoping her face didn't look like it might break, Eloise forced herself to do the same. She was too upset to analyse why she was pissed off.

Savannah held out a hand, motioning for Eloise to join her. When Eloise shook her head no, she shrugged and danced with Janelle instead.

They did a weird bump and grind, and Eloise's mood lifted. Her emotions were all over the place. Was she hormonal? No, that wasn't it.

In her gut, she knew Savannah and Carla had a history, and for the first time since they'd met, she felt jealous and insecure. She didn't like how that made her feel, sick to her stomach, and she didn't know how to deal with it either.

Chapter 24

Eloise pulled into the driveway. The outside light came on, illuminating the chilly night air. "Coming in?"

"I don't know. Am I?" Savannah asked.

"I would like it if you did."

"Sure." Her voice was clipped. The tension between them was so thick, Eloise was surprised she'd agreed to come inside at all.

She unlocked the door and let Savannah in first. "Coffee?"

"No, thanks." She sat at the table and Ratbag ran over as if she'd missed her friend. Stupid cat.

"Tea?"

"I'm fine, thanks. I'll be up peeing all night as it is."

"That's fine, I'm a heavy sleeper." *Hell of a way to test the waters, Eloise.*

"You expect me to stay?"

"I don't *expect* you to do anything."

"But you expect me to act a certain way?"

Frustrated, Eloise slid into the chair opposite Savannah at the kitchen table. She'd walked away from conflict for so long, she didn't know where to start with how she was feeling. "I don't know how to do this."

"That's my line," Savannah said, her expression devoid of emotion. "So why don't you just tell me what's bothering you?"

"You seriously need to ask?"

An eyebrow lifted.

"Carla."

"What about her?"

"Have you fucked her?" Eloise asked.

"No."

"Bullshit!"

Savannah stood. "I'll see myself out."

"No!" Eloise grabbed her arm, releasing it when Savannah looked down at her hand. "Sorry. I told you I don't know how to do this."

"Nor do I," Savannah said. "So now what?" She folded her arms, closing herself off.

"Let's try." Eloise flicked on the living room light, relieved when Savannah followed. They sat on the sofa.

"I'm going to start by telling you why I got upset." Eloise said, feeling stupid now. "It was clear to me you and Carla have a past."

"We all have a past, Eloise."

She normally loved the way her name rolled off Savannah's tongue, but not tonight. She said it like it tasted bitter.

"You knew this might happen."

"Not at my best mate's house," Eloise said.

"Taupō is small. You and I both know that. Town, then the café. I'm sitting in the home of a kid I see three times a week. You don't think that's weird for me?"

"I suppose. But it was knowing you two have a history and then seeing her flirting like crazy." She looked away, her heart still heavy. "You looked really into Carla when you were dancing."

Savannah cupped her chin and gently turned Eloise's face to look at her. "I haven't fucked her. We used to dance together."

"Strip?" Eloise joined the dots.

"Correct." Savannah didn't bother denying it. She had no reason to, and that wasn't what was bothering Eloise.

"It was more than that. She kept giving me these smug looks. It's hard to explain."

"Not really." Savannah's gaze softened. "Carla's a pro at playing head games. Now that you've told me, I can practically see her playing us off, and I'm sorry I didn't pick up on that."

Although she should drop it, Eloise pressed on. "She followed you to the bathroom."

"That surprised me too. Especially since she didn't appear to want Frank to know we knew each other, which I was happy to play along with."

"What about the workplace romance comment?" That was when her mind had spiralled down the rabbit hole. She'd put two and two together and come up with six.

"It was a dig."

"So she doesn't know about Libellule's?" Eloise's head was spinning. She was no longer sure what was up and what was down, and she'd only had two drinks all night.

"I didn't say that, but I'm not at liberty to say more. The only thing I can tell you emphatically is that I haven't slept with her."

"I believe you."

"Good. But that hasn't fixed the bigger problem, has it?" Savannah crossed an ankle over her knee, her posture rigid again.

"What?" Eloise dared to ask, wishing she hadn't acted like a child and sulked in the first place. Then they wouldn't be having this conversation.

"You said you are fine with what I do, but clearly, you're not. What happens next time I cross paths with someone who has used Libellule's services?"

She considered that for a moment. It hadn't bothered her before — the thought of it, talking about it, asking how Savannah's day was — so why now?

"Do they all act like Carla?" She'd wanted to get a rise out of Eloise, and what bothered her most was she'd let her.

"No. Most of the time you wouldn't know. Like the woman who breezed past us when we had a drink at the bar."

"Really?!" Although they'd been surrounded by people that night, her sole focus had been on Savannah. Even if someone had tipped their head in acknowledgement, she wouldn't have noticed.

"Really." The first hint of a smile made an appearance. "But I was there with you, just like tonight."

She stretched an arm along the back of the sofa and waggled her fingers, motioning Eloise to come closer.

She burrowed into her side, looking at the embers glowing in the bottom of the fire. "I'm sorry for acting like an insecure nelly."

"I'm sorry for not being more aware." Savannah lifted Eloise's chin.

Their eyes locked seconds before their lips met. It felt good; not only to be kissing but to have a conversation like two adults, exchanging heartfelt words rather than tossing slurs back and forth that ended in a heated argument.

The kiss grew heavy, and before long they were both breathing hard.

"Do you still have the rope I gave you?" Savannah asked when they came up for air.

"Of course."

"Go get it."

"Ooh," Eloise joked. "Is this like angry sex?"

"Are you still angry?"

"No," Eloise said, feeling like she'd made a big deal out of nothing. "I wasn't angry. I just felt insecure."

"Then let me help you feel...secure. Actually." Savannah paused, her smile growing. "Never mind."

"Fuck that." Eloise sprang up off the sofa. Savannah had planted the seed and her flower was dripping with nectar. *Fuckin hell, El. Terrible analogy.*

"Counting," Savannah said as she stood and slipped out of her jacket.

"Wood's by the fire. Feel free to stoke it," Eloise called over her shoulder as she bolted up the stairs.

"Believe me, I intend to stoke the fire."

When Eloise stepped back onto the landing, her breath stalled. While she'd been fart-arsing around in her room, digging the rope out from under her clothes, Savannah had ditched her jeans and top.

She stood in the middle of the living room looking as sexy as ever, wearing a burgundy bra and matching briefs. As Eloise descended the stairs, she let her gaze roam over her body—her black hair flowing over her shoulders, her belly button piercing, her sleeve of tattoos, and back up to her alluring green eyes.

Holding her gaze captive, Savannah took the rope from her. "Strip."

In record time, she was naked and unsure what was hotter. The warmth radiating off the fire or the heated look in Savannah's eyes.

"You're stunning."

"Thank you, Mistress." For most of her life, she'd never thought of herself as anything other than average, but when she was with Savannah, she always felt beautiful. The urge to dive under the blankets and turn out the lights was a thing of the past.

Savannah guided them over to the sofa and sat, motioning for Eloise to sit between her legs. She slid onto the sofa, relishing in the warm cocoon of Savannah's thighs and the feel of Savannah's lips on her neck.

She tipped her head to the side, giving her better access.

"Scoot forward and put your arms behind your back."

Glad they'd only had two drinks, Eloise obeyed. If they'd had more, this wouldn't be happening. Savannah was too responsible for that. She held onto her thumb with one hand, and wiggled her fingers, grazing them over the lace of Savannah's briefs.

"Brat." Her tone was playful. "Grab your elbows."

Smiling to herself, she moved position, surprised how restrained she felt before Savannah even started weaving the rope through her arms, around her biceps and back again.

"Does this mean I'm into BDSM?" Eloise asked.

The term had always held a scary connotation to her. It evoked images of whips and chains, spanking and canes, red marks and welts. The only part that had ever appealed to her was bondage and discipline, and even then, her limits were pitiful.

"If you're referring to enjoying bondage, I guess you could say yes. But just because you enjoy the B of BDSM doesn't mean you're into all of it. And some people who are into rope play aren't into BDSM at all."

"How does that work?" She'd always thought the two were tied. Pardon the pun.

Savannah looped the rope through her arms again. "This is how I see it but don't quote me." A flicker of red rope flashed in the corner of Eloise's eye before it was pulled in again. "Bondage cages—"

Her eyes went wide. "Say what?"

"Bondage cages—slave cage, kitty cage, puppy cage. Google it sometime, it's fascinating."

"Pass." The word came easily, but the curious side of her would check it out. It might not be for her, but that didn't mean she wasn't open to finding out what the appeal was to others.

Savannah slipped a finger under the rope and pulled. "Not too tight?"

"No."

"Good. Back to what I was saying, there are many ways to restrain a sub. But Japanese bondage, shibari, rope play, call it what you will, is more about the journey of getting there."

That made sense. Just like the last time they'd used rope, Eloise was slipping into a blissful sense of serenity.

"And as in any practice where you give up control of your body to someone else, as long as there is communication and trust, it can be intensely intimate and fulfilling."

She trusted Savannah beyond the shadow of a doubt, and tonight they'd proved they could communicate even when the topic was uncomfortable.

"Do you trust me, Eloise?"

"Yes, Mistress."

"Do you feel secure?" she whispered in Eloise's ear, the meaning of her words loud and clear.

"Yes, Savannah." That part was about them as a couple, not a game of give and take. And she hated that she'd let the green-eyed monster get its claws into her. "I'm sorry about earl—"

"Shh." Savannah snaked her hands around and cupped Eloise's breasts. "No more talk." She teased her nipples into hard buds.

Basking in the sensations coursing through her body, Eloise leaned back, resting her head against Savannah and opening herself up to her.

"Fuck," Eloise gasped when Savannah wet a finger and circled her clit.

"I intend to." The sultry timbre of her voice made Eloise throb with anticipation.

***

It was after midnight by the time they made it upstairs and fell into bed, completely naked with Ratbag trying to insert herself between them.

"When was the last time you slept with someone?" Savannah asked, scratching Ratbag under the chin. The cat's earlier behaviour still had Eloise perplexed.

"Last month." Her reply made Savannah's eyes go wide. Eloise laughed. "Mackenzie and I were watching a movie. She fell asleep."

"The movie was that good, huh?"

"Must've been." Needing to get closer, Eloise scooted Ratbag to the foot of the bed and shuffled over. "Other than my daughter, you're the only person who's slept in this bed."

"You didn't fight Anton for your marital bed?" She poked Eloise in the side.

"Stop." Laughing, she grabbed her finger. "Remember when you said you had an opinion about Mackenzie having a relationship with her father?"

Savannah nodded.

"I'd like to know what that is."

"Do you think it would be good for her mental health?"

That was a no-brainer. "Right now, no."

"Then don't force the issue. Family or not, some relationships are toxic. I don't know many parents who would blackmail their child, and I know fewer who would hide a pet from them."

"That was pretty low," Eloise said.

"And calculated."

She wasn't wrong, and Eloise was glad to be away from all of that. She stared into Savannah's soulful, green eyes. "Thank you for being here." For a minute there, she'd thought the night wasn't going to end well.

"Thank me in the morning. If I don't keep you awake all night."

"Do you snore?"

"Not that I know of, but I tend to sleep diagonally, so I apologise in advance."

"Just don't push me out." Eloise flicked off the lamp and they gravitated towards one another, legs entwined, arms draped across waists.

"Did you hear Janelle's invite as we left?"

"No," Eloise said into the darkness. She'd smiled and waved and done all the right things to indicate she'd had a rip-roaring night, but she'd been tone-deaf, too wrapped up in the misery of her own making. "Invite where?"

"To the mount. Skiing next weekend."

"What?" Her eyes had started to droop, but she was wide awake again now.

"Don't you want to go?" Savannah asked. "I thought it would be a good way for Mackenzie to see us together on neutral ground."

That was a really good point, and a really bad suggestion on Janelle's part. If she knew her best friend, though, it had also been intentional. She was going to make damn sure Eloise made good on her word that she might join them this year.

Chapter 25

Eloise gripped the rail at the bottom of the stairs and called out, "Hurry up, girls, or we'll be late."

Mackenzie descended the stairs with Bobby on her tail. "Like you care if we're late."

"Please don't."

"Sorry." Mackenzie gave her an apologetic smile. She turned to Bobby. "Mum's terrified of the gondola. Dad used to freak her out."

"Oh, you do have a father," Bobby teased, eyes full of mischief.

Mackenzie shrugged. "Yeah, well, you know what they say about family."

It was tempting to join in and make a joke about not doing a very good job of picking her father, but then Mackenzie wouldn't be Mackenzie, and Eloise wouldn't change a thing.

"Don't worry," Bobby said to Eloise. "Ms Sloane will look after you." She gave her a goofy grin as if the news that they were dating would never get old.

Right on nine a.m., there was a knock at the door. Eloise rushed to grab it, but Mackenzie skidded in front of her.

"Wait." She picked up Ratbag. "Okay."

She'd seen her and would've nudged her aside, but Mackenzie was a tad overprotective of her fur baby. She dumped her on the sofa in the living room and ran back.

"Okay. Go."

Everyone piled out the door at once, and Eloise took the opportunity to fake-stumble, falling straight into Savannah's arms. "Hey, you."

"Hey yourself." Savannah pecked her on the lips.

"Gross." Mackenzie shielded her eyes as she sauntered past.

The side door on Savannah's van opened, and Leilani ushered Bobby and Mackenzie into the back. They climbed in and the door slid closed, leaving them alone in the cold.

"I think I'll have some more of that." Savannah kissed her once again, then opened the front passenger door for Eloise.

"Shit. Two secs."

"It takes me longer than that."

Laughing, Eloise pointed a finger in jest. "Behave." She ran back to the house and locked it.

Once they were on the road, introductions were made to Leilani and her boyfriend, Tyson, who looked perfectly at home amidst three teenage girls.

It was a crisp, clear day with barely a cloud in the sky. There were warnings to take care on the icy roads, which only added to Eloise's anxiety. She hadn't told Savannah exactly how nervous she was about today.

Hopefully, everyone's excitement would rub off on her, and she would forget to freak out when they were hovering above the ground, relying on a cable to keep them alive.

"No Jack?" Savannah asked.

"No. He's hanging out with his mates." Although it was Eloise's weekend with him, once again he'd texted to say he was busy, which was a shame because she would've liked him to meet Savannah today.

She could've put her foot down and told him he had to come along, but there was no point introducing them when he was under duress. Besides, there were plenty more weekends ahead of them, and once winter sports finished, they would have even more free time.

"How old is he?" Savannah asked.

"Just turned fifteen."

"I was sixteen last month," Mackenzie piped up from the back seat. "I'm still accepting presents."

"Mackenzie!" Eloise shot her a look over her shoulder.

"It was a joke." Her eyes sparkled. "But I'm still accepting presents."

Savannah glanced in the rear-view mirror. "How about cake? Will that do?"

"You don't have—" Eloise started to say, but the barely perceptible shake of Savannah's head stopped her.

"She makes the best pineapple upside-down cake," Leilani said.

"That will work." Bobby tipped her head upside down like a goof.

***

It was almost eleven by the time they made it to the mount. Janelle, Grant and the boys were already waiting for them.

"Have you been here long?" Eloise asked as they caught up to them at the entrance.

Everyone was dressed for the weather—thick jackets, hats, gloves, and waterproof pants. Some had snowboards, others had skis. Eloise had neither. Just making it to the top would be a massive achievement.

Janelle gave her a kind smile. "You okay?"

"If I don't think about it." Her stomach tried to turn itself inside out.

"Where's Jack?" Liam asked. They'd always got along well.

"He had something else on."

"Weird." He shrugged as if pondering what could possibly be better than spending a day on the slopes.

As a group, they made their way over to the self-service kiosks at the base of the ski field. Happy to stand back, Eloise let everyone else go first, scanning their QR codes and retrieving a plastic card pass from the machine.

"Cold?" Savannah asked.

"No. Why?" It was icy, but the sun was out and her jacket was toasty warm.

"You look like you're frozen to the spot."

"Oh." She laughed to hide her embarrassment. "Just waiting my turn."

"Want me to do yours, Mum?" Mackenzie asked when Eloise's legs refused to work.

"No, I can do it." She put one foot in front of the other, feeling like she had blocks of ice glued to her feet.

"Woohoo. Let's go." Six teens took off for the ski lifts.

"See you at the top," Grant said, dragging Janelle to a lift.

What the fuck? Eloise froze. What happened to going up on the gondola? At least that was enclosed.

"You okay?" Savannah eyed her with concern.

"No." She wanted to cry. "I'm fucking terrified."

Savannah took her hands in her own. "Breathe."

She inhaled and exhaled, blowing out misty air.

"Again."

She obeyed, and her heart stopped trying to beat its way out of her chest.

"Scared of heights?"

"No. Of falling."

"I'm not going to patronise you and say it's all in your mind, but—"

"It's all in my mind," she supplied, doing her best to put thoughts of her demise aside. "Will you hold my hand?" At least if she died, it wouldn't be all bad.

"I'll do one better. I'll catch you if we fall." Savannah tucked a lock of Eloise's hair under her woollen hat. "I'm taller than you, so I'll hit the ground first. You can land on top of me."

"Sounds like fun." Eloise waggled her eyebrows.

"Ready?"

Her glee fled. "Do or die, right?"

"We're not going to die."

They joined the queue, and Eloise screamed like a little girl when the chair swooped under her backside and scooped them up. They were airborne.

"Look." Savannah pointed to the nearby mountain peaks. "That's Mount Tongariro." She swept her arm sideways. "And Ngauruhoe—more famously known as Mount Doom from *Lord of the Rings*."

The lift shuddered, sending a spike of terror through Eloise. She gripped the bar until her knuckles hurt. They were probably white, but she couldn't see them through her gloves.

"It's okay." Savannah put a hand on her thigh. "We're almost there."

Wow, they were too. And they hadn't fallen to their deaths. It wasn't until she got off and stared down the snow-covered mountain that it struck her they had to get down again.

"Isn't it beautiful?" Savannah asked, glancing around the ski field.

Numerous people were making the most of the clear, blue, chilly day. Some were goofing around, having snow fights. Others were skiing and snowboarding.

Grant skidded to a stop next to Janelle. "Ready?"

She flipped her goggles into place, dug her ski poles in and was off, streaking ahead of Grant. Liam and Tyler followed their parents, whooping as they went.

Bobby and Mackenzie grabbed their snowboards and did some fancy moves. It looked exhilarating, but that didn't mean Eloise was in any hurry to give it a try.

Hands buried in her pockets, she stood there, feeling like a spare cow in a milking shed. What the hell was she supposed to do? Lean against a rail and wait until everyone was done?

There was no rail, so she bounced on her toes to keep warm. Before long, her nerves had abated and she was smiling, the excitement in the air seeping into her.

When everyone headed in the direction of Happy Valley, she followed.

"Time for you to get in on the action," Savannah said, holding onto a yellow sled.

"No way!" Eloise looked down the hill. "I'm not ready to die." A bit dramatic, but going downhill with no brakes? Not happening.

"It'll be a blast," Mackenzie said, looking far more excited by the prospect than Eloise.

"We'll be cheering you on." Janelle gave her a reassuring smile.

"You're supposed to be my friend." She harrumphed to hide exactly how terrified she felt right then.

How hard could it be? Kids were sledding and skiing. No broken bones. At least, not that she'd witnessed.

As if sensing her anxiety, or more likely reading her body language, Savannah squeezed her shoulder. "It's okay. We don't have to do this. We can walk down."

"No!" Rather than feel like an arsehole for ruining Savannah's fun, she did what she'd done from the day she met her. Put her trust in her hands. "I'll be okay."

She eyed Eloise closely. "Are you sure?"

Eloise nodded. Feeling like she might throw up, she stepped aside as Savannah positioned the sled near the edge of the hill and climbed on.

She scooted back and spread her legs. "Get on." She patted the spot in front of her.

Certain she looked like the biggest coward on earth, Eloise glanced at all the eyes on her. She waited for the ridicule but none came. All she received were reassuring nods, kind smiles and a mouthed "You've got this" from Mackenzie.

Gingerly, she got into place, the cold of the sled seeping through her clothes. Savannah pulled her back until she was nestled between her thighs.

"Put your arms over my legs."

She did as she was told, and Savannah wrapped her arms around Eloise's waist, making her feel secure.

"Lean back and make sure you keep your feet up." Savannah tightened her arms, her face pressed against Eloise's cheek.

Then they were sailing down the hill, the wind whipping around them, their feet in the air. The world fell away, until it was just the two of them.

Adrenaline kicked in, and Eloise cried out "Wahoo!" as they flew down the slope.

They slowed at the bottom, sliding along the even ground towards a snowbank. Eventually, they came to a stop, breathing hard from the rush.

The shouts of Mackenzie and Bobby rang in her ears as they came to a stop beside them. Beaming, Mackenzie held out a hand, and Eloise high-fived her.

"You okay?" Savannah rubbed her hands up and down Eloise's arms as if to make sure she was still in one piece.

Elated, Eloise leaned back against her. "That was…" She was at a loss for words. "Awesome."

Janelle skidded to a stop, skis kicking up snow. "Well?" She flicked her goggles up. "How was it?"

"Amazing." She jumped off the sled. "Let's do it again."

Laughing, everyone climbed the hill and zoomed back down again. When they'd all had enough, they took the gondola to Knoll Ridge Chalet — New Zealand's highest dining experience — and replenished their reserves with hot drinks and toasted sandwiches.

Whether it was the company, the panoramic views, or because she'd conquered a fear, the two-kilometre ride to the top was the icing on the cake of a fabulous day out. Instead of sitting there full of terror like she'd feared, she'd laughed and joked and snuggled into Savannah's side.

At two thousand and twenty metres above sea level, life was looking pretty damn good.

Chapter 26

Eloise read Jack's message for a second time, her heart sinking. Had the axe she'd been waiting to fall finally dropped? The last couple of weekends he was supposed to stay, he'd had one excuse after another for why he couldn't. The first time she hadn't thought much of it. Now, though, it was impossible not to join the dots.

He hadn't stayed since she'd told him about Savannah. He'd been fine when she came out to him a month ago. There'd been none of his tell-tale signs when something made him uncomfortable. No grinning and bearing it with an insincere smile.

"Have you talked to your brother lately?" Eloise asked Mackenzie.

The curtains were drawn, the fire was blazing, and a casserole was simmering in the crockpot. By the time she dished up at six, the meat would be falling off the lamb shanks.

"Yep," Mackenzie said. "Well, not talked, but texted."

"Did he tell you he's not coming over?"

"Mm-hmm." She burrowed into the beanbag as if she wanted it to swallow her, but Eloise wasn't letting up.

She leaned forward on the sofa, elbows on her knees. "Do you know why?"

Mackenzie shrugged, eyes glued to the television.

"Mackenzie, look at me."

"What?" She sounded both irritated and resigned.

"Talk to me, please." It sounded like a plea—a desperate plea—and to an extent, it was.

"Fine. He thinks it's gross that you're dating my soccer coach. There. Now you know."

Even though she'd suspected as much, it was still a blow. She slumped against the sofa. A furball lodged in her lower back and she lurched forward again.

Giving her the stink eye, Ratbag crawled out and jumped off. Eloise had been so intent on getting to the bottom of what was going on with Jack, she hadn't seen her.

What had changed? Was he worried she was going to turn up at his school, arm in arm with a woman, and ruin his reputation?

"Is it school? His mates?" she asked Mackenzie, who kept her eyes on Ratbag as she climbed into her lap.

"I don't know."

The realisation that her son didn't feel like he could talk to her burned a hole in her heart. Was this how Anton felt when Mackenzie shunned him? Was karma biting her in the arse? No, that couldn't be it. She'd done nothing wrong.

Distraught, she jammed her elbows on her knees and cradled her head in her hands. Her kids meant the world to her. She'd always said she would do anything for them, but maybe it was time to redefine *anything*.

One thing she wouldn't do was compromise her future happiness for a child who had as good as flown the nest anyway. She'd taught both of her kids that communication was key, and it was time to take some of her own advice. Eloise hit mute on the remote.

"Text your brother. Tell him you really, really want him to come over."

"No." Mackenzie set her mouth in a tight line, her defiance making Eloise take a good look at herself.

She'd almost fallen into Anton's trap of using the kids like chess pieces. "I'm sorry. I'm just hurting."

Sadness washed over Mackenzie's features. She plucked at Ratbag's fur, still not meeting Eloise's gaze. "I'm sorry too, but Jack used to try to talk me into going to Dad's, and it pissed me off, so I swore never to do that to him."

"I know." Even though she felt like she might shatter, Eloise pushed to her feet. "Hungry?"

"Not really," Mackenzie said.

"Me either. Should we have a popcorn night and watch a movie?"

Mackenzie's head snapped up. "But it's a school night."

"I won't tell if you won't."

**

The following day, after signing out of work at three, Eloise headed in the direction of the school and parked a block away.

Feeling like a cop on a stakeout, she slid down in the driver's seat.

The second she spotted Jack ambling along the street, hands in his pockets, her heart rate spiked.

Graduating from amateur cop to kidnapper, she cracked open the car door and peered over the roof. "Hey, son. Would you like a ride home?"

His face dropped, but he quickly recovered, playing her at her own game with a huge, insincere smile. "Nah, I'm good. Nice day to walk."

"I'm going to the doughnut shop."

"Nah, I'm good." He was almost past the car, and his mates were looking at him like he was crazy for turning down doughnuts.

"I'll have yours." Logan rushed over to the car and grabbed the door handle.

"Move it." Jack nudged him aside.

Logan slid into the front, and Jack climbed in the back with Finn. He was the same age as Jack and almost twice his size. He also played a mean game of rugby.

Having three teenage boys in the car wasn't ideal for talking to Jack, but she could cross one theory off her list. His peers weren't the issue.

She hadn't planned on eating doughnuts, but that was exactly what happened. After dropping Logan home and then Finn, she finally had her son to herself.

The wall he'd erected between them was so thick, he might as well have hung a blanket between them. A block from the house, she pulled over and shut off the engine.

"Wanna tell me what's going on?"

He folded his arms so tightly, she expected to hear a rib crack. "Nothing."

"Don't lie to me. You know you can talk to me about anything."

He remained silent, staring out the windscreen.

"Is this about Savannah?" She spoke in a soft tone, coaxing him to open up.

His nostrils flared, eyes straight ahead.

She tried again. "Is it because Savannah is Mackenzie's soccer coach?" Hopefully, she hadn't just dumped Mackenzie in it for telling her that piece of information.

"Sick."

"Being gay isn't an illness, Jack. You know that. And I didn't know Savannah was Mackenzie's soccer coach when we met." She stared at the side of his head. "Look at me, please."

As if it pained him to look at her head-on, he turned no more than an inch.

"What's this really about? Talk to me."

Finally, he swivelled to face her. The look of contempt twisting his features was unnerving. When had her sweet, fun-loving child turned into a young man full of hatred?

"You're doing this to hurt Dad! You turned Mackenzie against him, and now you're trying to make him look like a loser to his mates."

At that moment, she knew exactly where this loathing was coming from. Those weren't the words of her son. They were Anton's words. The bastard was still using him like a pawn in a chess game. But this wasn't a game. Feelings and lives were involved.

She swallowed the anger that had climbed up her throat, tasting it, savouring it, committing it to memory for the person who deserved her fury.

"I've only ever done what's right by you kids."

"Then you should've stayed with Dad instead of busting up the family. I miss Mackenzie."

That stung. Boy did it sting. But there was no going back, so she had to find a way forward.

"You know being gay isn't a bad thing. Mackenzie is dating a girl." She winced, ashamed with herself for going straight for Jack's soft spot, but the words bounced off him.

"That won't last. She's only doing it to be like you."

More of Anton's words, and it was starting to piss her off. "Is that what Dad said?"

"Yes." His eyes went big. "No."

"It's okay, son. You don't have to tell me, but you are old enough to make up your own mind. Are there any gay kids at your school?"

"Of course. There's an LGBTQ-something-something group. I can't remember all the letters. They're cool."

"How do you think they'd feel if you said they would get over it?"

He grinned, some of the Jack she knew shining through. "I'd probably get a punch in the nose."

"Lucky for you, your sister would never strike you. But she's really into Bobby. She's not doing it just to be like me. You should know that." Mackenzie had never done anything to be just like her mother. She was a strong, independent young woman.

"I suppose." He was backing down, but confusion still knitted his brow. "It's just hard. Sometimes I don't know what to believe. Mackenzie hates Dad, and I don't know why." He glanced up, peering through his hair that was in need of a cut. "And it *is* kind of weird you're dating her coach. Imagine if Dad started dating my rugby coach."

"I don't think you'll have to worry about that." She ruffled his hair, both because she needed to touch him and because he hated it. "Mackenzie thought it was weird at first, too, but she also understands I didn't set out to hurt anyone. Least of all your father."

"But you did."

Fucking bastard. She doubted that, but he'd made Jack believe it. "Well, I'm sorry about that, but I can't control his feelings." A thought jumped into her head, and she ran with it, jumping tracks like an out-of-control train. "Is Dad seeing anyone?"

"I'm not allowed to talk about it."

Of course he wasn't, but she could turn that to her advantage. "Then how about you don't tell Dad what I'm up to, and then you won't get caught in the middle? Instead, you'll be able to make up your own mind."

He nodded, deep in thought. "I guess that's fair."

"Now you're sounding like a fifteen-year-old." She started the car. "Let me get you home."

"Is she coming over this weekend?"

"Who?"

"That lady."

She laughed. "Her name's Savannah. And yes, I was going to invite her over." It was on the tip of her tongue to say she wouldn't if he didn't want her to, but what kind of precedent would that be setting? "I was going to see if her niece wants to come over too. Leilani. She's pretty."

He gave her a coy smile.

"So you'll come over?"

His smile fell. "Maybe next weekend." He breathed out a heavy sigh. "Dad will be pissed."

Fucking cunt. It wasn't a word she used lightly, but she was getting tired of hearing his name. They didn't even live in the same house and she was still cleaning up his bullshit.

"I'll talk to him."

"No." Jack spun around, hand on the door as Eloise came to a stop two doors down from home. His home.

"I know what he says isn't right. But he gets in my head and then everything gets confused. I'm sorry."

"Me too." She hated her kids were going through this, being apart, adulting way before their time, dealing with the pile of shit their father kept heaping on them. "If you need me, I'm only ever a phone call away."

"Or a text."

"Or that."

He opened the car door. "Thanks for the doughnuts."

"You're welcome."

She wanted to hug him, but she didn't think they were there yet, so she stayed put, hands gripping the steering wheel. The door closed, and she watched him wander along the street, school bag over his shoulder.

When he turned and waved, smiling widely, her heart soared. They were going to be okay.

Chapter 27

By the time spring arrived, Eloise had been formally introduced to Savannah's mum, Pearl, and hung out with her on the sideline during most soccer games. She was every bit as awesome as her daughter, and the love she felt for both Savannah and Leilani was palpable. And pride!

Eloise had listened intently when Pearl told her how proud she was of Savannah for all of her achievements: her dedication to soccer—something that had been her sister's first love—becoming a coach, obtaining a Certificate in Beauty Therapy and another for pedicures and manicures.

It'd been hard not to smile when Pearl informed her the only man you could rely on was a manicure. But that wasn't why Eloise was standing outside Libellule's, staring at the neon-blue door.

When she stood here five months ago, she'd had no idea it would lead to love, and it was the most wonderful feeling in the world.

She could've used the back entrance, but she didn't want to tip Savannah off and ruin the element of surprise. Like the first time she'd been here, she knocked and waited. Adrenaline kicked in, making her heart race.

The door opened and a familiar face, Ruby from memory, welcomed her inside. "Hello. Please, come in."

"Thanks." She glanced over her shoulder before entering. No one was paying her any attention, and even if they were, she could simply be there for a manicure.

"Lois?"

"Correct." She'd used a new alias so Savannah wouldn't click if she read the appointment book.

Even if she didn't, surely the staff were given the names of the clients they were about to become intimately acquainted with.

The door from the back of the business to the front opened, and a woman with shoulder-length brown hair and an air of authority entered. "Everything okay out here?"

"Fine, boss," Ruby said. "I'm just about to take her through."

"I can do that." The woman extended a hand. "I'm Soraya. Savannah's boss."

"Nice to meet you." And why did she have the distinct feeling Soraya knew she was more than a client to Savannah?

Had she confided in her boss about Eloise? Even if she had, how would Soraya know what Eloise looked like?

"Don't overthink it." Soraya gave her a kind smile.

They stopped outside door number two. "Do you want to do the honours, or should I?"

"I can," Eloise said softly. Her nerves were firing on all cylinders as it was, and she didn't need an audience.

Alone again, Eloise blew out a breath and knocked.

The door clicked open, and Savannah's jaw almost hit the floor. "Eloise?" She grabbed her by the arm and yanked her into the room. "What are you doing here?"

That was a good question. She'd wanted to come here today and do what she'd planned to do the very first time she'd come here. Be a good submissive, but right off the bat, she was fumbling.

"I wanted to surprise you."

"Well, you've certainly done that." She stared, eyebrows pinched. "What's going on?"

Doing her best to slip into the role of submissive, Eloise cleared her mind of all thoughts. "I have an appointment."

"Okay." Savannah stared at Eloise, looking completely lost.

"For the hour I'm here, I want you to treat me like a client."

"Okay." She straightened her spine. "Give me a minute." She turned her back, and Eloise took the opportunity to admire the tight fit of her corset dress. It was bright red, laced up the back, and accentuated every delicious curve.

By the time Savannah turned back around, she was all business. "Limits?"

"No butt stuff."

They'd talked about sex and kink often enough that she didn't feel like she had to spell anything else out.

Savannah might push her, but she couldn't imagine her crossing any lines. Like strapping up. Maybe one day, but right now, being penetrated with a cock, no matter how far removed the appendage was from a man, was not something she craved.

"Any others?" She searched Eloise's eyes, a hint of uncertainty lingering in the green depths.

"No. I trust you."

"Good, because I would never abuse that trust." She picked up a paddle and tapped it against the flat of her palm. It was black vinyl with a fluffy red heart in the middle. What would it feel like against her skin?

Eyeing her up and down, Savannah tapped a toe. "Present yourself."

The authoritative tone of her voice was like the flip of a switch, turning them from two women on equal footing to a beautiful power exchange based on mutual respect.

Eloise ditched her clothes and stood with her hands behind her back, chest thrust out. Thanks to Savannah, she'd learned to love her body. All of it, the jiggly bits and her large nipples she used to hate.

"Safe word?"

"Pickles."

"Good girl." Savannah moved to the cross in the corner. "Hands here." She tapped the top two points. Feet here." She nudged the bottom with her foot.

A quiver of anticipation shot through Eloise as Savannah secured her wrists and ankles, the leather cuffs cool against her skin. The first time she stood against the Saint Andrew's cross, she was afraid she would freak out if Savannah restrained her, but this time she felt empowered. It wasn't a feeling of power over her dominant. It was conquering the fear she'd let get the better of her last time.

A blindfold slid into place and she closed her eyes, tuning into the scents and sounds around her. The rustle of something behind her. The citrusy aroma coming from the incense burner in the corner.

Savannah trailed her fingers down Eloise's back, leaving a trail of gooseflesh in her wake. "Have you been a bad girl?"

"Yes, Mistress. I've been very bad."

The paddle hit her left butt cheek. "Have you been playing with yourself without permission?" Another strike; this one firmer.

"Yes, Mistress. I came three times. But I was thinking about you."

"Brat." The next strike landed with purpose.

It stung, but surprisingly, it made Eloise crave more. "Thank you, Mistress. Please may I have another?" She'd read that somewhere, and it sounded good to her ears.

"No, you may not." A thunk sounded and she pictured the paddle hitting the floor.

Certain Savannah wasn't done with her, she waited, and waited, and waited some more. Not for the first time, Savannah's comment about testing who really had all the power ran through her mind.

Her breath feathered over Eloise's neck. "I think you need a good flogging."

Ohmigod, ohmigod, ohmigod. Could she do this? Should she safe word? No, she couldn't do that.

This was one of the things she'd said she would like to explore the first time she was here. And she had. Sort of. But she'd been so uncertain, Savannah had taken it easy on her, barely grazing the strands over her flesh.

"Don't make me ask again," Savannah said as she ran the handle of the flogger down Eloise's spine, bumping over her vertebrae.

"Yes, Mistress. I need to be punished." That wasn't something she'd ever have expected to come out of her mouth, but the words felt natural, like she'd said them countless times before.

The strands of the flogger slashed across her backside. The crack echoed around the room, but the blow didn't hurt anywhere near as much as the internet would have you believe. Not that she watched porn. Oh, who was she kidding? She'd been watching lesbian porn for longer than she could remember.

The flogger made contact for a third time, clearing her mind. The strike had more weight, making her muscles jump and her flesh heat.

"Colour?"

"Green, Mistress." Right then, she felt like she could take a lot more. Restrained and blindfolded, she felt relaxed, confident, safe and sexy.

"You're beautiful."

"Thank you, Mis—" The next lash made her buck against the restraints. Before she recovered, another one landed, and then the flogger hit the floor.

"Good girl." Savannah released Eloise's wrists and lowered her arms to her sides. "Do you know what good girls get?" The seductive purr of her voice and her warm breath on Eloise's neck made her quiver.

"Orgasms?"

"If you beg for it."

"Please, Mistress."

"Nice try." Savannah's fingers ghosted over Eloise's breasts, pinching her nipples until every tweak was like a caress over her clit. When Savannah finally took a nipple into her mouth, Eloise tipped her head back with a groan of pleasure.

Then all play stopped. "Are you seeing the picture?"

"I'm seeing the back of the blindfold."

"Would you like to find out how the twisted loop spanking cane feels?"

"Ah, nah, I'm good."

"But that's the thing, Eloise…" She twisted a nipple, making Eloise rise up on her toes. "You're not being a good girl. You're being a brat."

"Sorry, Mistress." The pressure eased, and she dropped from the balls of her feet to her heels. "Let me make it up to you." She went to step away from the cross, but the cuffs wrapped around her ankles pulled tight, reminding her that although her hands were free, she was still restrained.

"I'm going to free your ankles because I don't want you to fall on your face, but you are not to touch without permission, understood?"

"Yes, Mistress."

Oh, God. Her brain stalled and a rush of heat pooled between her thighs when something slick and wet slid between her legs, back and forth, between her labia, along her clit. Smooth. Slippery. Intoxicating.

When it started to pulse, she gasped, hand flying out to grab onto Savannah before she came to her senses and lowered it again. A throaty chuckle emanated from deep within Savannah's chest, and an image of her smiling face flashed through Eloise's mind.

The torment continued, driving her higher and higher.

"Pinch your nipples."

"Yes, Mistress." She squeezed the sensitive buds at the same time as she squeezed her eyes shut. She probably looked like she was in pain, and that wasn't far from the truth. She was a hot ball of fire, ready to combust.

"Close."

The vibrations stopped, and she cursed under her breath, pulling another chuckle from Savannah. "Poor baby. Do you want to come?"

"Yes."

"Then beg for it."

"Please, Mistress. Please let me come."

"Why should I?" The vibrations started again. And stopped.

Beyond frustrated, it took all of Eloise's willpower not to stamp her foot. "Because I've been a good girl."

It was worth a try, but in reality, she'd done nothing but stand there, following Savannah's orders. Ah, she got it. Or more specifically, she'd done it. "Because I've been a good submissive."

"You have." She sealed her mouth over Eloise's, then the vibrator was back. It was hard to kiss and pant, but she loved the connection.

As her breathing became more frantic, chest heaving, thighs soaked, Savannah broke the lip-lock, but not their connection.

The vibrator stopped, replaced by Savannah's hand. She cupped Eloise's mound, massaging her clit with the flat of her hand.

Then, gently, exactly how Eloise liked it, she slipped a finger inside and curled it forward, and that was it. The touch propelled her straight into an orgasmic bliss so intense, she toppled forward, legs giving out.

Savannah's strong arms wrapped around her. "I've got you."

She guided her over to the chair, removed the blindfold, and wrapped a blanket around Eloise's shoulders.

"Hot." She pushed it off, blinking against the light bulb burning her eyeballs. Or maybe that was the bead of sweat that ran down her forehead and dripped in her eye.

"Drink." A bottle of water appeared in her hand. She gulped greedily, not quite ready to come down but aware she'd probably used up most of her hour.

Savannah squatted before her, hand on Eloise's knee. "How do you feel?"

"Amazing." She felt high...and naked. Very naked. She didn't have a stitch of clothing on, and Savannah was still clothed. It made the power exchange all the more potent. "What about you?"

"Surprised." She handed Eloise her clothes and helped her dress. "Lois, huh?"

"Yep." She laughed. What a ridiculous name.

"I'm flattered."

"Huh?"

"Lois Lane. I guess that makes me your superwoman."

"Oh, right. Yep, you got it." That wasn't why she'd picked the name, but now she was glad she had. "You're my hero."

"You're my train."

"Trainwreck." She laughed, unsure how to take the comment and equally unsure why she couldn't stop giggling like a five-year-old.

"No." Savannah shook her head, not a hint of laughter in her eyes. "Bad analogy, if that's what you call it. But I meant the light at the end of my tunnel. Oh, God. That must be the lamest thing I've ever said." She slapped a hand over her forehead, and they started laughing, then they were hugging, then they were kissing.

"I love you," Eloise said, her breath stalling as time stood still. Was it too much? When Savannah didn't say anything, she laughed nervously. "See? Trainwreck."

"You're nothing of the sort." Was that a tear in her eye? "From the day you walked through that door, I felt something."

"Me?" Eloise joked, slicing through the tension.

"Yes, you. But what I felt was more than physical." Her gaze was as soft as her smile. "You were a bundle of nervous energy, eager to please, and—"

"Scared shitless," Eloise interrupted.

"And that," Savannah said, a hint of vulnerability appearing before she continued. "I wanted to please you as much as you wanted to please me."

"And you did," Eloise assured her.

Although she hadn't taken charge in the way Eloise had mapped out, she'd still commanded the scene, and she'd done it in a way that left Eloise flying high. In fact, she was yet to come down.

"Despite having never met before, we just gelled," Savannah said. "I had a hard time putting you out of my mind, but I was also aware it would be foolhardy to pursue a client."

"Then fate interjected," Eloise said.

"To an extent, I suppose so. But it was more than that. We had chemistry right from the start. Without that, we still would've crossed paths but continued walking in opposite directions."

"But we didn't," Eloise said fiercely, hating the thought of it.

Savannah pulled her close, and Eloise melted into her, absorbing her heat and heart. Savannah kissed the top of her head. "I didn't think I was capable of a romantic relationship, but you taught me otherwise."

Eloise removed her head from under Savannah's chin and met her gaze. "Is that your way of saying you love me?"

"Yes, Eloise Carter. I love you. Happy now?" There was that heart-stopping smile Eloise would never tire of.

"Extremely." She stood on tippytoes and kissed Savannah softly. "So very happy."

Epilogue

"Remind me again how I got roped into this?" Savannah asked.

There was no rope in sight, but every time she said something like that, it transported Eloise back to the day Savannah introduced her to rope bondage. And she shouldn't be thinking about sex with twenty teenagers nearby.

It was Mackenzie's eighteenth birthday party, and she'd invited half of the soccer team over and a few other friends from school. The guys were outnumbered two to one but didn't seem to mind.

"What do you mean roped in? It's payback for when you dragged me to the pools to help supervise ten girls."

"I think you got the better end of the deal." Savannah poured a litre of orange juice into the virgin punch.

In the afternoon, while Mackenzie had been out for lunch with Jack, they'd decorated the garage with balloons and streamers. For a nice touch, Savannah had installed some coloured bulbs. They were operated by a remote and ranged in colour from yellow to red to blue.

Mackenzie bounced inside, a ball of energy, cheeks rosy pink, beanie on. "Are the sausage rolls ready?"

Bobby appeared next, letting in another blast of cold air. "Do you need a hand?"

"Nope, we've got it," Savannah said.

She grabbed the mitts and pulled the tray of sausage rolls out of the oven. Steam rose off them, filling the kitchen with the aroma of sausage meat, onion, mixed herbs and golden pastry.

"Wait up." Eloise slid two onto a plate.

With a peck on the lips, Savannah headed for the door, tray in hand. Mackenzie playfully gagged and followed.

"Just for that, I'm coming too." She'd promised to give Mackenzie her space, but as a responsible host, she'd been popping in and out of the garage, making sure everyone was behaving.

Unbeknownst to Mackenzie, she'd also phoned most of the kids' parents to inform them alcohol would be available. Not a single one minded.

Eloise put the virgin punch on the table they'd set up with chips, dips, and finger foods. "Punch anyone?"

Casey wandered over. "Is there alcohol in it?"

"No, sorry."

"Cool. Can I have a glass, please?"

Eloise picked up the ladle and filled a plastic cup for Casey. She'd dropped out of the team last year due to her mother being unwell. "How have you been?"

"Good, thanks."

"How's Mum?" Eloise didn't want to pry, but she did care. For any teenager to become caregiver to a parent had to be tough.

"She's okay. The medication helps." Clasping her cup in both hands, she sipped. She looked so fragile, Eloise wanted to tuck her under her wing and protect her like a frightened bird.

"That's good to hear."

"Casey!" three girls called out. "Come dance."

A huge smile lit her face. "Sorry." She dumped the half-empty cup and bolted.

Eloise smiled to herself. She'd been hesitant about the party, but it was great to see so many teenagers interacting without their phones.

Savannah sidled up behind her and slid an arm around Eloise's waist. "When are we doing the cake?"

She leaned back against her. "Mackenzie will hate me."

"She'll act all butt hurt, but she'll love it."

Over the past week, they'd hashed out what kind of cake to make for her. A cake Mackenzie said she didn't want because she wasn't doing any stupid speeches. Her words.

"I guess now is as good a time as any." Some of the teens were leaving around ten, and it would be a shame if they missed out.

Back in the house, Eloise retrieved the cake she'd stashed. It made her smile, but she wasn't so sure Mackenzie would agree. They could blame Leilani for the suggestion, but they'd promised not to throw her under the bus.

"Should we light the candle first?" Savannah asked.

"Yep." It was cold outside, freezing actually, but there wasn't even the hint of a breeze.

Savannah grabbed the empty cardboard box they'd packed the groceries in earlier in the day. "Scissors?"

"Now?" Eloise burst out laughing. Was it lame to laugh at your own joke? Probably. And she probably wasn't as funny as she thought she was either.

"Move." Savannah bumped her out of the way, a small smile playing across her lips. "I'll get them myself."

Working together, they cut one side of the box out, sat the cake inside, and lit the candle—a number eighteen.

The box worked well, adding to the suspense when they entered the garage. Savannah caught Leilani's eye and sliced her hand across her throat, signalling for her to kill the music.

Two girls continued to dance, but everyone else retreated to the bench seats placed along the walls. Savannah tapped the two stragglers on the shoulders and they took their seats.

Mackenzie and Bobby were on the opposite side of the garage, and even though they were ten feet away, Eloise could see the suspicion in her eyes.

"Come here, please," Eloise mouthed.

Mackenzie hung her head, staring at her Ugg boots. Bobby pushed her to her feet and gave her a shove. "Get up there, birthday girl."

"Yeah!" a chorus of voices rang out.

"I said no cake," she hissed under her breath when she reached Eloise's side.

"I know, but your friends might want some."

"Is it chocolate?"

"Sort of," Eloise bit back a smile.

"Should I be worried?"

"Not at all," Savannah said with a straighter face than Eloise could've managed. "But you should thank your friends for coming today."

Mackenzie turned and faced them. "Thank you for coming tonight." Her voice was flat.

Bobby cupped her hands around her mouth. "Speech!"

Mackenzie shot daggers at her with her eyes. She'd never enjoyed being the centre of attention, so maybe it'd been unfair of Eloise to expect her to front up.

"Cake!" Eloise called out, taking the attention off Mackenzie. "Who wants cake?"

"Wait," Mackenzie said. "I have to think of a wish." She closed her eyes, and you could've heard a pin drop. Everyone fell silent as if they might be able to hear her thoughts.

The second she opened them, her mates wanted to know what she was going to wish for.

"It's bad luck to tell anyone," one of the guys informed everyone.

"That's an old wives' tale," Mackenzie said. "But that's what I hope for…" She turned to Eloise and Savannah, love shining in her eyes. "For mum to be a wife again."

Oh my God, did she just give us her blessing if we choose to get married? Eloise's exuberance was quickly replaced by embarrassment. They'd never talked about anything of the sort. What they had now worked fine. Would this change things, make Savannah feel like she had to propose? Fuck! Was she waiting for Eloise to propose?

"Happy wife, happy life." Savannah pecked her on the cheek and everyone cheered.

Flustered, Eloise turned to the box. She couldn't get into what Mackenzie said with twenty teenagers looking at them. As she held onto the tray, Savannah slid the box back, revealing the cake.

Bobby rushed forward for a closer look. "Ha-ha. That's the best."

"You think!" Mackenzie narrowed her eyes, but it didn't mask the sparkle in them.

"Read it," Eloise said.

"What? The toilet paper?" Mackenzie had already moved around the cake, which was a giant roll of toilet paper with chocolate cupcakes around it, decorated so they resembled smiling poop emojis.

Mackenzie read the words aloud, "Shit happens. Roll with it. Happy eighteenth." She blew out the candle.

Savannah handed her a knife, but before she could slice the cake, Eloise put a hand on her shoulders. "Now make a wish for you."

She closed her eyes briefly, then stabbed the knife into the middle of the white toilet roll, delighted when she saw the cake was also chocolate. How could a poop cake not be chocolate?

Bobby, who was still standing nearby, poked the middle of the cake. "Mm, feels nice and…moist."

Inappropriate, but damn, Eloise was going to miss her when she went to university next year. Over the last two years, she'd become a fixture in their home.

Once the giggles quieted down, Eloise started singing Happy Birthday and everyone joined in.

***

As soon as the last teen was picked up, Eloise fell into bed with Savannah. Not long after, they heard Mackenzie and Bobby stumble in. They were full of cheer, but thankfully everyone had been well-behaved and no one had got trashed. Eighteen was the legal drinking age in New Zealand, but that didn't mean she would let them go wild. Not on her watch.

Next year, when Mackenzie went off to Massey University in Palmerston North—three hours away—Eloise wouldn't have any control over how much she drank, but she was a smart kid and hopefully wouldn't go too crazy.

"How are you feeling?" Savannah snuggled up to her side.

"Shouldn't I be asking you that?" Eloise pulled the blankets higher, tucking them under her chin.

"Compared to soccer drills, this was a walk in the park. Now, tell me how you're feeling."

"Embarrassed." Eloise bit her lip. "I don't know where Mackenzie got that idea in her head from."

The bedside light reflected in Savannah's eyes as she pulled Eloise closer. Eloise basked in the feel of skin on skin, their tummies and breasts aligning.

"What idea?" Savannah asked.

"You know what I mean." Even after two years together, there were still times she felt bashful around Savannah. And alive. And aroused. Hell, Savannah gave her all the feels.

"Oh, the happy wife comment." She studied Eloise closely. "Are you happy?"

"Very." Since meeting Savannah, her days were so much brighter. Even when life threw her a shit sandwich, she found something to smile about.

"Do you need to be married to be happy?"

"God, no." The response came without thought.

"Good. But if you ever decide you do, let me know."

"Oh, great. So it's on my shoulders, is it?"

Savannah lifted one shoulder, raising the blankets and letting a chill slip beneath the sheets. "I think when that time comes, we'll both know."

That was true, and Eloise had learned a signed piece of paper didn't guarantee a lifetime of happiness. The commitment they had to each other went deeper than that.

"I love you, Savannah Sloane."

"And I you, Eloise Sloane."

"Hey, who said I'd take your name?"

"Me." She poked Eloise in the side, and a tussle broke out. Stark naked, Savannah flung the blankets back and straddled Eloise's waist, poking her sides until she was laughing and bucking and begging her to stop.

A bang on the wall brought an abrupt stop to the torment.

"Ew. Are you guys doing it?"

"Goodnight, Mackenzie."

"Goodnight, Mum."

Printed in Great Britain
by Amazon

41141583R10155